THE WAYS OF WHITE FOLKS

THE WAYS OF
WHITE FOLKS

Langston Hughes

VINTAGE BOOKS
A Division of Random House
New York

ISBN: 0-394-71304-4

Manufactured in the United States of America

23456789B

VINTAGE BOOKS EDITION,
November 1971

TO NOEL SULLIVAN

The ways of white folks,
I mean some white folks. . . .

BERRY.

Thanks are due the editors of ESQUIRE, THE AMERICAN MERCURY, SCRIBNER'S, OPPORTUNITY, THE BROOKLYN DAILY EAGLE, DEBATE, and ABBOTT'S MONTHLY for permission to reprint certain of these stories first published in their pages.

CONTENTS

I.	CORA UNASHAMED	3
II.	SLAVE ON THE BLOCK	19
III.	HOME	32
IV.	PASSING	49
V.	A GOOD JOB GONE	54
VI.	REJUVENATION THROUGH JOY	66
VII.	THE BLUES I'M PLAYING	96
VIII.	RED-HEADED BABY	121
IX.	POOR LITTLE BLACK FELLOW	129
X.	LITTLE DOG	156
XI.	BERRY	171
XII.	MOTHER AND CHILD	183
XIII.	ONE CHRISTMAS EVE	192
XIV.	FATHER AND SON	200

CORA UNASHAMED

Melton was one of those miserable in-between little places, not large enough to be a town, nor small enough to be a village—that is, a village in the rural, charming sense of the word. Melton had no charm about it. It was merely a nondescript collection of houses and buildings in a region of farms—one of those sad American places with sidewalks, but no paved streets; electric lights, but no sewage; a station, but no trains that stopped, save a jerky local, morning and evening. And it was 150 miles from any city at all—even Sioux City.

Cora Jenkins was one of the least of the citizens of Melton. She was what the people referred to when they wanted to be polite, as a Negress, and when they wanted to be rude, as a nigger—sometimes adding the word "wench" for no good reason, for Cora was usually an inoffensive soul, except that she sometimes cussed.

She had been in Melton for forty years. Born there. Would die there probably. She worked for the Studevants, who treated her like a dog. She stood it. Had to stand it; or work for poorer white folks who would treat her worse; or go jobless. Cora was like a tree—once rooted, she stood, in spite of storms and strife, wind, and rocks, in the earth.

She was the Studevants' maid of all work—washing, ironing, cooking, scrubbing, taking care of kids, nursing old folks, making fires, carrying water.

Cora, bake three cakes for Mary's birthday tomorrow night. You Cora, give Rover a bath in that tar soap I bought. Cora, take Ma some jello, and don't let her have even a taste of that raisin pie. She'll keep us up all night if you do. Cora, iron my stockings. Cora, come here . . . Cora, put . . . Cora . . . Cora . . Cora! Cora!

And Cora would answer, "Yes, m'am."

The Studevants thought they owned her, and they were perfectly right: they did. There was something about the teeth in the trap of economic circumstance that kept her in their power practically all her life—in the Studevant kitchen, cooking; in the Studevant parlor, sweeping; in the Studevant backyard, hanging clothes.

You want to know how that could be? How a trap could close so tightly? Here is the outline:

Cora was the oldest of a family of eight children —the Jenkins niggers. The only Negroes in Melton, thank God! Where they came from originally —that is, the old folks—God knows. The kids were born there. The old folks are still there now: Pa drives a junk wagon. The old woman ails around the house, ails and quarrels. Seven kids are gone. Only Cora remains. Cora simply couldn't go, with nobody else to help take care of Ma. And before that she couldn't go, with nobody to see that her brothers and sisters got through school (she the oldest, and Ma ailing). And before that—well, somebody had to help Ma look after one baby behind another that kept on coming.

As a child Cora had no playtime. She always had a little brother, or a little sister in her arms. Bad, crying, bratty babies, hungry and mean. In the eighth grade she quit school and went to work with the Studevants.

After that, she ate better. Half day's work at first, helping Ma at home the rest of the time. Then full days, bringing home her pay to feed her father's children. The old man was rather a drunkard. What little money he made from closet-cleaning, ash-hauling, and junk-dealing he spent mostly on the stuff that makes you forget you have eight kids.

He passed the evenings telling long, comical lies to the white riff-raff of the town, and drinking licker. When his horse died, Cora's money went for a new one to haul her Pa and his rickety wagon around. When the mortgage money came due, Cora's wages kept the man from taking the roof from over their heads. When Pa got in jail, Cora borrowed ten dollars from Mrs. Studevant and got him out.

Cora stinted, and Cora saved, and wore the Studevants' old clothes, and ate the Studevants' left-over food, and brought her pay home. Brothers and sisters grew up. The boys, lonesome, went away, as far as they could from Melton. One by one, the girls left too, mostly in disgrace. "Ruinin' ma name," Pa Jenkins said, "Ruinin' ma good name! They can't go out berryin' but what they come back in disgrace." There was something about the cream-and-tan Jenkins girls that attracted the white farm hands.

Even Cora, the humble, had a lover once. He came to town on a freight train (long ago now), and worked at the livery-stable. (That was before autos got to be so common.) Everybody said he was an I. W. W. Cora didn't care. He was the first man and the last she ever remembered wanting. She had never known a colored lover. There weren't any around. That was not her fault.

This white boy, Joe, he always smelt like the horses. He was some kind of foreigner. Had an accent, and yellow hair, big hands, and grey eyes.

It was summer. A few blocks beyond the Studevants' house, meadows and orchards and sweet fields stretched away to the far horizon. At night, stars in the velvet sky. Moon sometimes. Crickets and katydids and lightning bugs. The scent of grass. Cora waiting. That boy, Joe, a cigarette spark far off, whistling in the dark. Love didn't take long

—Cora with the scent of the Studevants' supper about her, and a cheap perfume. Joe, big and strong and careless as the horses he took care of, smelling like the stable.

Ma would quarrel because Cora came home late, or because none of the kids had written for three or four weeks, or because Pa was drunk again. Thus the summer passed, a dream of big hands and grey eyes.

Cora didn't go anywhere to have her child. Nor tried to hide it. When the baby grew big within her, she didn't feel that it was a disgrace. The Studevants told her to go home and stay there. Joe left town. Pa cussed. Ma cried. One April morning the kid was born. She had grey eyes, and Cora called her Josephine, after Joe.

Cora was humble and shameless before the fact of the child. There were no Negroes in Melton to gossip, and she didn't care what the white people said. They were in another world. Of course, she hadn't expected to marry Joe, or keep him. He was of that other world, too. But the child was hers— a living bridge between two worlds. Let people talk.

Cora went back to work at the Studevants'—coming home at night to nurse her kid, and quarrel with Ma. About that time, Mrs. Art Studevant had a child, too, and Cora nursed it. The Studevants' little girl was named Jessie. As the two children began to walk and talk, Cora sometimes brought Josephine to play with Jessie—until the Studevants objected, saying she could get her work done better if she left her child at home.

"Yes, m'am," said Cora.

But in a little while they didn't need to tell Cora to leave her child at home, for Josephine died of whooping-cough. One rosy afternoon, Cora saw the little body go down into the ground in a white casket that cost four weeks' wages.

Since Ma was ailing, Pa, smelling of licker, stood with her at the grave. The two of them alone. Cora was not humble before the fact of death. As she turned away from the hole, tears came—but at the same time a stream of curses so violent that they made the grave-tenders look up in startled horror.

She cussed out God for taking away the life that she herself had given. She screamed, "My baby! God damn it! My baby! I bear her and you take her away!" She looked at the sky where the sun was setting and yelled in defiance. Pa was amazed and scared. He pulled her up on his rickety wagon and drove off, clattering down the road between green fields and sweet meadows that stretched away to the far horizon. All through the ugly town Cora wept and cursed, using all the bad words she had learned from Pa in his drunkenness.

The next week she went back to the Studevants. She was gentle and humble in the face of life—she loved their baby. In the afternoons on the back porch, she would pick little Jessie up and rock her to sleep, burying her dark face in the milky smell of the white child's hair.

II

The years passed. Pa and Ma Jenkins only dried up a little. Old Man Studevant died. The old lady had two strokes. Mrs. Art Studevant and her husband began to look their age, greying hair and sagging stomachs. The children were grown, or nearly so. Kenneth took over the management of the hardware store that Grandpa had left. Jack went off to college. Mary was a teacher. Only Jessie remained a child—her last year in high-school. Jessie, nineteen now, and rather slow in her studies, graduating at last. In the Fall she would go to Normal.

Cora hated to think about her going away. In her heart she had adopted Jessie. In that big and careless household it was always Cora who stood like a calm and sheltering tree for Jessie to run to in her troubles. As a child, when Mrs. Art spanked her, as soon as she could, the tears still streaming, Jessie would find her way to the kitchen and Cora. At each school term's end, when Jessie had usually failed in some of her subjects (she quite often failed, being a dull child), it was Cora who saw the report-card first with the bad marks on it. Then Cora would devise some way of breaking the news gently to the old folks.

Her mother was always a little ashamed of stupid Jessie, for Mrs. Art was the civic and social leader of Melton, president of the Woman's Club three years straight, and one of the pillars of her church. Mary, the elder, the teacher, would follow with dignity in her footsteps, but Jessie! That child! Spankings in her youth, and scoldings now, did nothing to Jessie's inner being. She remained a plump, dull, freckled girl, placid and strange. Everybody found fault with her but Cora.

In the kitchen Jessie bloomed. She laughed. She talked. She was sometimes even witty. And she learned to cook wonderfully. With Cora, everything seemed so simple—not hard and involved like algebra, or Latin grammar, or the civic problems of Mama's club, or the sermons at church. Nowhere in Melton, nor with anyone, did Jessie feel so comfortable as with Cora in the kitchen. She knew her mother looked down on her as a stupid girl. And with her father there was no bond. He was always too busy buying and selling to bother with the kids. And often he was off in the city. Old doddering Grandma made Jessie sleepy and sick. Cousin Nora (Mother's cousin) was as stiff and prim as a minister's daughter. And Jessie's older brothers and sister went their ways, seeing Jessie hardly at all, except at the big table at mealtimes.

Like all the unpleasant things in the house, Jessie was left to Cora. And Cora was happy. To have a child to raise, a child the same age as her Josephine would have been, gave her a purpose in life, a warmth inside herself. It was Cora who nursed and mothered and petted and loved the dull little Jessie through the years. And now Jessie was a young woman, graduating (late) from high-school.

But something had happened to Jessie. Cora knew it before Mrs. Art did. Jessie was not too stupid to have a boy-friend. She told Cora about it like a mother. She was afraid to tell Mrs. Art. Afraid! Afraid! Afraid!

Cora said, "I'll tell her." So, humble and unashamed about life, one afternoon she marched into Mrs. Art's sun-porch and announced quite simply, "Jessie's going to have a baby."

Cora smiled, but Mrs. Art stiffened like a bolt. Her mouth went dry. She rose like a soldier. Sat down. Rose again. Walked straight toward the door, turned around, and whispered, "What?"

"Yes, m'am, a baby. She told me. A little child. Its father is Willie Matsoulos, whose folks runs the ice-cream stand on Main. She told me. They want to get married, but Willie ain't here now. He don't know yet about the child."

Cora would have gone on humbly and shamelessly talking about the little unborn had not Mrs.

Art fallen into uncontrollable hysterics. Cousin Nora came running from the library, her glasses on a chain. Old Lady Studevant's wheel-chair rolled up, doddering and shaking with excitement. Jessie came, when called, red and sweating, but had to go out, for when her mother looked up from the couch and saw her she yelled louder than ever. There was a rush for camphor bottles and water and ice. Crying and praying followed all over the house. Scandalization! Oh, my Lord! Jessie was in trouble.

"She ain't in trouble neither," Cora insisted. "No trouble having a baby you want. I had one."

"Shut up, Cora!"

"Yes, m'am. . . . But I had one."

"Hush, I tell you."

"Yes, m'am."

III

Then it was that Cora began to be shut out. Jessie was confined to her room. That afternoon, when Miss Mary came home from school, the four white women got together behind closed doors in Mrs. Art's bedroom. For once Cora cooked supper in the kitchen without being bothered by an interfering voice. Mr. Studevant was away in Des Moines. Somehow Cora wished he was home. Big and gruff as he was, he had more sense than the women. He'd probably make a shot-gun wedding out of it. But left to Mrs. Art, Jessie would never marry the Greek boy at all. This Cora knew. No man had been found yet good enough for sister Mary to mate with. Mrs. Art had ambitions which didn't include the likes of Greek ice-cream makers' sons.

Jessie was crying when Cora brought her supper up. The black woman sat down on the bed and lifted the white girl's head in her dark hands. "Don't you mind, honey," Cora said. "Just sit tight, and when the boy comes back I'll tell him how things are. If he loves you he'll want you. And there ain't no reason why you can't marry, neither —you both white. Even if he is a foreigner, he's a right nice boy."

"He loves me," Jessie said. "I know he does. He said so."

But before the boy came back (or Mr. Studevant either) Mrs. Art and Jessie went to Kansas City. "For an Easter shopping trip," the weekly paper said.

Then Spring came in full bloom, and the fields and orchards at the edge of Melton stretched green and beautiful to the far horizon. Cora remembered her own Spring, twenty years ago, and a great sympathy and pain welled up in her heart for Jessie, who was the same age that Josephine would have been, had she lived. Sitting on the kitchen porch shelling peas, Cora thought back over her own life—years and years of working for the Studevants; years and years of going home to nobody but Ma and Pa; little Josephine dead; only Jessie to keep her heart warm. And she knew that Jessie was the dearest thing she had in the world. All the time the girl was gone now, she worried.

After ten days, Mrs. Art and her daughter came back. But Jessie was thinner and paler than she'd ever been in her life. There was no light in her eyes at all. Mrs. Art looked a little scared as they got off the train.

"She had an awful attack of indigestion in Kansas City," she told the neighbors and club women. "That's why I stayed away so long, waiting for her to be able to travel. Poor Jessie! She looks healthy, but she's never been a strong child. She's one of the worries of my life." Mrs. Art talked a lot, explained a lot, about how Jessie had eaten the wrong things in Kansas City.

At home, Jessie went to bed. She wouldn't eat. When Cora brought her food up, she whispered, "The baby's gone."

Cora's face went dark. She bit her lips to keep from cursing. She put her arms about Jessie's neck. The girl cried. Her food went untouched.

A week passed. They tried to *make* Jessie eat then. But the food wouldn't stay on her stomach. Her eyes grew yellow, her tongue white, her heart acted crazy. They called in old Doctor Brown, but within a month (as quick as that) Jessie died.

She never saw the Greek boy any more. Indeed, his father had lost his license, "due to several complaints by the mothers of children, backed by the Woman's Club," that he was selling tainted ice-cream. Mrs. Art Studevant had started a campaign to rid the town of objectionable tradespeople and questionable characters. Greeks were bound to be one or the other. For a while they even closed up Pa Jenkins' favorite bootlegger. Mrs. Studevant thought this would please Cora, but Cora only said, "Pa's been drinkin' so long he just as well keep on." She refused further to remark on her employer's campaign of purity. In the midst of this clean-up Jessie died.

On the day of the funeral, the house was stacked with flowers. (They held the funeral, not at the church, but at home, on account of old Grandma Studevant's infirmities.) All the family dressed in deep mourning. Mrs. Art was prostrate. As the hour for the services approached, she revived, however, and ate an omelette, "to help me go through the afternoon."

"And Cora," she said, "cook me a little piece of ham with it. I feel so weak."

"Yes, m'am."

The senior class from the high-school came in a body. The Woman's Club came with their badges. The Reverend Doctor McElroy had on his highest collar and longest coat. The choir sat behind the coffin, with a special soloist to sing "He Feedeth His Flocks Like a Shepherd." It was a beautiful Spring afternoon, and a beautiful funeral.

Except that Cora was there. Of course, her presence created no comment (she was the family servant), but it was what she did, and how she did it, that has remained the talk of Melton to this day—for Cora was not humble in the face of death.

When the Reverend Doctor McElroy had finished his eulogy, and the senior class had read their memorials, and the songs had been sung, and they were about to allow the relatives and friends to pass around for one last look at Jessie Studevant, Cora got up from her seat by the dining-room door. She said, "Honey, I want to say something." She spoke as if she were addressing Jessie. She approached the coffin and held out her brown hands over the white girl's body. Her face moved in agitation. People sat stone-still and there was a long pause. Suddenly she screamed. "They killed you! And for nothin'. . . . They killed your child. . . . They took you away from here in the Springtime of your life, and now you'se gone, gone, gone!"

Folks were paralyzed in their seats.

Cora went on: "They preaches you a pretty sermon and they don't say nothin'. They sings you a song, and they don't say nothin'. But Cora's here, honey, and she's gone tell 'em what they done to you. She's gonna tell 'em why they took you to Kansas City."

A loud scream rent the air. Mrs. Art fell back in her chair, stiff as a board. Cousin Nora and sister Mary sat like stones. The men of the family rushed forward to grab Cora. They stumbled over wreaths and garlands. Before they could reach her, Cora pointed her long fingers at the women in black and said, "They killed you, honey. They killed you and your child. I told 'em you loved it, but they didn't care. They killed it before it was . . ."

A strong hand went around Cora's waist. Another grabbed her arm. The Studevant males half pulled, half pushed her through the aisles of folding chairs, through the crowded dining-room, out into the empty kitchen, through the screen door into the backyard. She struggled against them all the way, accusing their women. At the door she sobbed, great tears coming for the love of Jessie.

She sat down on a wash-bench in the backyard, crying. In the parlor she could hear the choir singing weakly. In a few moments she gathered herself together, and went back into the house. Slowly, she picked up her few belongings from the kitchen and pantry, her aprons and her umbrella, and went off down the alley, home to Ma. Cora never came back to work for the Studevants.

Now she and Ma live from the little garden they raise, and from the junk Pa collects—when they can take by main force a part of his meager earnings before he buys his licker.

Anyhow, on the edge of Melton, the Jenkins niggers, Pa and Ma and Cora, somehow manage to get along.

SLAVE ON THE BLOCK

THEY WERE PEOPLE who went in for Negroes—
Michael and Anne—the Carraways. But not in the
social-service, philanthropic sort of way, no. They
saw no use in helping a race that was already too
charming and naive and lovely for words. Leave
them unspoiled and just enjoy them, Michael and
Anne felt. So they went in for the Art of Negroes—
the dancing that had such jungle life about it, the
songs that were so simple and fervent, the poetry
that was so direct, so real. They never tried to influence that art, they only bought it and raved over
it, and copied it. For they were artists, too.

In their collection they owned some Covarrubias
originals. Of course Covarrubias wasn't a Negro,
but how he caught the darky spirit! They owned
all the Robeson records and all the Bessie Smith.
And they had a manuscript of Countee Cullen's.
They saw all the plays with or about Negroes, read
all the books, and adored the Hall Johnson Singers.
They had met Doctor DuBois, and longed to meet
Carl Van Vechten. Of course they knew Harlem
like their own backyard, that is, all the speakeasies

and night clubs and dance halls, from the Cotton Club and the ritzy joints where Negroes couldn't go themselves, down to places like the Hot Dime, where white folks couldn't get in—unless they knew the man. (And tipped heavily.)

They were acquainted with lots of Negroes, too —but somehow the Negroes didn't seem to like them very much. Maybe the Carraways gushed over them too soon. Or maybe they looked a little like poor white folks, although they were really quite well off. Or maybe they tried too hard to make friends, dark friends, and the dark friends suspected something. Or perhaps their house in the Village was too far from Harlem, or too hard to find, being back in one of those queer and expensive little side streets that had once been alleys before the art invasion came. Anyway, occasionally, a furtive Negro might accept their invitation for tea, or cocktails; and sometimes a lesser Harlem celebrity or two would decorate their rather slow parties; but one seldom came back for more. As much as they loved Negroes, Negroes didn't seem to love Michael and Anne.

But they were blessed with a wonderful colored cook and maid—until she took sick and died in her room in their basement. And then the most marvellous ebony boy walked into their life, a boy as black as all the Negroes they'd ever known put together.

"He *is* the jungle," said Anne when she saw him.
"He's 'I Couldn't Hear Nobody Pray,'" said
Michael.

For Anne thought in terms of pictures: she was a
painter. And Michael thought in terms of music:
he was a composer for the piano. And they had a
most wonderful idea of painting pictures and com-
posing music that went together, and then having a
joint "concert-exhibition" as they would call it.
Her pictures and his music. The Carraways, a sonata and a picture, a fugue and a picture. It would
be lovely, and such a novelty, people would have to
like it. And many of their things would be Negro.
Anne had painted their maid six times. And
Michael had composed several themes based on the
spirituals, and on Louis Armstrong's jazz. Now here
was this ebony boy. The essence in the flesh.

They had nearly missed the boy. He had come,
when they were out, to gather up the things the
cook had left, and take them to her sister in Jersey.
It seems that he was the late cook's nephew. The
new colored maid had let him in and given him the
two suitcases of poor dear Emma's belongings, and
he was on his way to the Subway. That is, he was in
the hall, going out just as the Carraways, Michael
and Anne, stepped in. They could hardly see the
boy, it being dark in the hall, and he being dark,
too.

"Hello," they said. "Is this Emma's nephew?"

"Yes'm," said the maid. "Yes'm."

"Well, come in," said Anne, "and let us see you. We loved your aunt so much. She was the best cook we ever had."

"You don't know where *I* could get a job, do you?" said the boy. This took Michael and Anne back a bit, but they rallied at once. So charming and naive to ask right away for what he wanted.

Anne burst out, "You know, I think I'd like to paint you."

Michael said, "Oh, I say now, that would be lovely! He's so utterly Negro."

The boy grinned.

Anne said, "Could you come back tomorrow?"

And the boy said, "Yes, indeed. I sure could."

The upshot of it was that they hired him. They hired him to look after the garden, which was just about as big as Michael's grand piano—only a little square behind the house. You know those Village gardens. Anne sometimes painted it. And occasionally they set the table there for four on a spring evening. Nothing grew in the garden really, practically nothing. But the boy said he could plant things. And they had to have some excuse to hire him.

The boy's name was Luther. He had come from the South to his relatives in Jersey, and had had only one job since he got there, shining shoes for a Greek in Elizabeth. But the Greek fired him because the boy wouldn't give half his tips over to the proprietor.

"I never heard of a job where I had to pay the boss, instead of the boss paying me," said Luther. "Not till I got here."

"And then what did you do?" said Anne.

"Nothing. Been looking for a job for the last four months."

"Poor boy," said Michael; "poor, dear boy."

"Yes," said Anne. "You must be hungry." And they called the cook to give him something to eat.

Luther dug around in the garden a little bit that first day, went out and bought some seeds, came back and ate some more. They made a place for him to sleep in the basement by the furnace. And the next day Anne started to paint him, after she'd bought the right colors.

"He'll be good company for Mattie," they said. "She claims she's afraid to stay alone at night when we're out, so she leaves." They suspected, though, that Mattie just liked to get up to Harlem. And they thought right. Mattie was not as settled as she looked. Once out, with the Savoy open until three in the morning, why come home? That was the way Mattie felt.

In fact, what happened was that Mattie showed Luther where the best and cheapest hot spots in Harlem were located. Luther hadn't even set foot in Harlem before, living twenty-eight miles away,

as he did, in Jersey, and being a kind of quiet boy.
But the second night he was there Mattie said,
"Come on, let's go. Working for white folks all day,
I'm tired. They needn't think I was made to answer
telephones all night." So out they went.

Anne noticed that most mornings Luther would
doze almost as soon as she sat him down to pose, so
she eventually decided to paint Luther asleep. "The
Sleeping Negro," she would call it. Dear, natural
childlike people, they would sleep anywhere they
wanted to. Anyway, asleep, he kept still and held
the pose.

And he *was* an adorable Negro. Not tall, but with
a splendid body. And a slow and lively smile that
lighted up his black, black face, for his teeth were
very white, and his eyes, too. Most effective in oil
and canvas. Better even than Emma had been. Anne
could stare at him at leisure when he was asleep.
One day she decided to paint him nude, or at least
half nude. A slave picture, that's what she would do.
The market at New Orleans for a background. And
call it "The Boy on the Block."

So one morning when Luther settled down in his
sleeping pose, Anne said, "No," she had finished
that picture. She wanted to paint him now repre-
senting to the full the soul and sorrow of his people.
She wanted to paint him as a slave about to be sold.
And since slaves in warm climates had no clothes,
would he please take off his shirt.

Luther smiled a sort of embarrassed smile and took off his shirt.

"Your undershirt, too," said Anne. But it turned out that he had on a union suit, so he had to go out and change altogether. He came back and mounted the box that Anne said would serve just then for a slave block, and she began to sketch. Before luncheon Michael came in, and went into rhapsodies over Luther on the box without a shirt, about to be sold into slavery. He said he must put him into music right now. And he went to the piano and began to play something that sounded like Deep River in the jaws of a dog, but Michael said it was a modern slave plaint, 1850 in terms of 1933. Vieux Carré remembered on 135th Street. Slavery in the Cotton Club.

Anne said, "It's too marvellous!" And they painted and played till dark, with rest periods in between for Luther. Then they all knocked off for dinner. Anne and Michael went out later to one of Lew Leslie's new shows. And Luther and Mattie said, "Thank God!" and got dressed up for Harlem.

Funny, they didn't like the Carraways. They treated them nice and paid them well. "But they're too strange," said Mattie, "they makes me nervous."

"They is mighty funny," Luther agreed.

They didn't understand the vagaries of white folks, neither Luther nor Mattie, and they didn't want to be bothered trying.

"I does my work," said Mattie. "After that I don't want to be painted, or asked to sing songs, nor nothing like that."

The Carraways often asked Luther to sing, and he sang. He knew a lot of southern worksongs and reels, and spirituals and ballads.

> *"Dear Ma, I'm in hard luck:*
> *Three days since I et,*
> *And the stamp on this letter's*
> *Gwine to put me in debt."*

The Carraways allowed him to neglect the garden altogether. About all Luther did was pose and sing. And he got tired of that.

Indeed, both Luther and Mattie became a bit difficult to handle as time went on. The Carraways blamed it on Mattie. She had got hold of Luther. She was just simply spoiling a nice simple young boy. She was old enough to know better. Mattie was in love with Luther.

At least, he slept with her. The Carraways discovered this one night about one o'clock when they went to wake Luther up (the first time they'd ever done such a thing) and ask him if he wouldn't sing his own marvellous version of John Henry for a man who had just come from Saint Louis and was sailing for Paris tomorrow. But Luther wasn't in his own bed by the furnace. There was a light in Mattie's room, so Michael knocked softly. Mattie said, "Who's that?" And Michael poked his head in, and here were Luther and Mattie in bed together!

Of course, Anne condoned them. "It's so simple and natural for Negroes to make love." But Mattie, after all, was forty if she was a day. And Luther was only a kid. Besides Anne thought that Luther had been ever so much nicer when he first came than he was now. But from so many nights at the Savoy, he had become a marvellous dancer, and he was teaching Anne the Lindy Hop to Cab Calloway's records. Besides, her picture of "The Boy on the Block" wasn't anywhere near done. And he did take pretty good care of the furnace. So they kept him. At least, Anne kept him, although Michael said he was getting a little bored with the same Negro always in the way.

For Luther had grown a bit familiar lately. He smoked up all their cigarettes, drank their wine, told jokes on them to their friends, and sometimes even came upstairs singing and walking about the house when the Carraways had guests in who didn't share their enthusiasm for Negroes, natural or otherwise.

Luther and Mattie together were a pair. They quite frankly lived with one another now. Well, let that go. Anne and Michael prided themselves on being different; artists, you know, and liberal-minded people—maybe a little scatter-brained, but then (secretly, they felt) that came from genius.

They were not ordinary people, bothering about the liberties of others. Certainly, the last thing they would do would be to interfere with the delightful simplicity of Negroes.

But Mattie must be giving Luther money and buying him clothes. He was really dressing awfully well. And on her Thursday afternoons off she would come back loaded down with packages. As far as the Carraways could tell, they were all for Luther.

And sometimes there were quarrels drifting up from the basement. And often, all too often, Mattie had moods. Then Luther would have moods. And it was pretty awful having two dark and glowering people around the house. Anne couldn't paint and Michael couldn't play.

One day, when she hadn't seen Luther for three days, Anne called downstairs and asked him if he wouldn't please come up and take off his shirt and get on the box. The picture was almost done. Luther came dragging his feet upstairs and humming:

> *"Before I'd be a slave*
> *I'd be buried in ma grave*
> *And go home to my Jesus*
> *And be free."*

And that afternoon he let the furnace go almost out.

That was the state of things when Michael's mother (whom Anne had never liked) arrived from

Kansas City to pay them a visit. At once neither Mattie nor Luther liked her either. She was a mannish old lady, big and tall, and inclined to be bossy. Mattie, however, did spruce up her service, cooked delicious things, and treated Mrs. Carraway with a great deal more respect than she did Anne.

"I never play with servants," Mrs. Carraway had said to Michael, and Mattie must have heard her.

But Luther, he was worse than ever. Not that he did anything wrong, Anne thought, but the way he did things! For instance, he didn't need to sing now all the time, especially since Mrs. Carraway had said she didn't like singing. And certainly not songs like "You Rascal, You."

But all things end! With the Carraways and Luther it happened like this: One forenoon, quite without a shirt (for he expected to pose) Luther came sauntering through the library to change the flowers in the vase. He carried red roses. Mrs. Carraway was reading her morning scripture from the Health and Life.

"Oh, good morning," said Luther. "How long are you gonna stay in this house?"

"I never liked familiar Negroes," said Mrs. Carraway, over her nose glasses.

"Huh!" said Luther. "That's too bad! I never liked poor white folks."

Mrs. Carraway screamed, a short loud, dignified scream. Michael came running in bathrobe and

pyjamas. Mrs. Carraway grew tall. There was a
scene. Luther talked. Michael talked. Anne appeared.

"Never, never, never," said Mrs. Carraway,
"have I suffered such impudence from servants—
and a nigger servant—in my own son's house."

"Mother, Mother, Mother," said Michael. "Be
calm. I'll discharge him." He turned on the non-
chalant Luther. "Go!" he said, pointing toward the
door. "Go, go!"

"Michael," Anne cried, "I haven't finished 'The
Slave on the Block.'" Her husband looked non-
plussed. For a moment he breathed deeply.

"Either he goes or I go," said Mrs. Carraway,
firm as a rock.

"He goes," said Michael with strength from his
mother.

"Oh!" cried Anne. She looked at Luther. His
black arms were full of roses he had brought to put
in the vases. He had on no shirt. "Oh!" His body
was ebony.

"Don't worry 'bout me!" said Luther. "I'll go."

"Yes, we'll go," boomed Mattie from the doorway, who had come up from below, fat and bel-
ligerent. "We've stood enough foolery from you
white folks! Yes, we'll go. Come on, Luther."

What could she mean, "stood enough"? What
had they done to them, Anne and Michael wondered. They had tried to be kind. "Oh!"

"Sneaking around knocking on our door at night," Mattie went on. "Yes, we'll go. Pay us! Pay us! Pay us!" So she remembered the time they had come for Luther at night. That was it.

"I'll pay you," said Michael. He followed Mattie out.

Anne looked at her black boy.

"Good-bye," Luther said. "You fix the vases."

He handed her his armful of roses, glanced impudently at old Mrs. Carraway and grinned—grinned that wide, beautiful, white-toothed grin that made Anne say when she first saw him, "He looks like the jungle." Grinned, and disappeared in the dark hall, with no shirt on his back.

"Oh," Anne moaned distressfully, "my 'Boy on the Block'!"

"Huh!" snorted Mrs. Carraway.

HOME

WHEN THE BOY CAME BACK, there were bright stickers and tags in strange languages the home folks couldn't read all over his bags, and on his violin case. They were the marks of customs stations at far-away borders, big hotels in European cities, and steamers that crossed the ocean a long way from Hopkinsville. They made the leather-colored bags and black violin case look very gay and circus-like. They made white people on the train wonder about the brown-skinned young man to whom the baggage belonged. And when he got off at a village station in Missouri, the loafers gathered around in a crowd, staring.

Roy Williams had come home from abroad to visit his folks, his mother and sister and brothers who still remained in the old home town. Roy had been away seven or eight years, wandering the world. He came back very well dressed, but awfully thin. He wasn't well.

It was this illness that had made Roy come home, really. He had a feeling that he was going to die, and he wanted to see his mother again. This feeling about death had been coming over him gradually for two or three years now. It seemed to him that it must have started in Vienna, that gay but dying city in Central Europe where so many people were hungry, and yet some still had money to buy champagne and caviar and women in the night-clubs where Roy's orchestra played.

But the glittering curtains of Roy's jazz were lined with death. It made him sick to see people fainting in the streets of Vienna from hunger, while others stuffed themselves with wine and food. And it made him sad to refuse the young white women trailing behind him when he came home from work late at night, offering their bodies for a little money to buy something to eat.

In Vienna Roy had a room to himself because he wanted to study and keep up his music. He studied under one of the best violin teachers. But it was hard to keep beautiful and hungry women out of his place, who wanted to give themselves to a man who had a job because in turn the man might let them sleep in his room, or toss them a few bills to take home to their starving parents.

"Folks catch hell in Europe," Roy thought. "I never saw people as hungry as this, not even Negroes at home."

But it was even worse when the orchestra moved back to Berlin. Behind the apparent solidity of that great city, behind doors where tourists never passed, hunger and pain were beyond understanding. And the police were beating people who protested, or stole, or begged. Yet in the cabaret where Roy played, crowds of folks still spent good gold. They laughed and danced every night and didn't give a damn about the children sleeping in doorways outside, or the men who built houses of packing boxes, or the women who walked the streets to pick up trade.

It was in Berlin that the sadness weighed most heavily on Roy. And it was there that he began to cough. One night in Prague, he had a hemorrhage. When he got to Paris, his girl friend took care of him, and he got better. But he had all the time, from then on, that feeling that he was going to die. The cough stayed, and the sadness. So he came home to see his mother.

He landed in New York on the day that Hoover drove the veterans out of Washington. He stayed a couple of days in Harlem. Most of his old friends there, musicians and actors, were hungry and out of work. When they saw Roy dressed so well, they asked him for money. And at night women whispered in the streets, "Come here, baby! I want to see you, darlin'."

"Rotten everywhere," Roy thought. "I want to go home."

That last night in Harlem, he couldn't sleep. He

thought of his mother. In the morning he sent her a telegram that he was on his way.

II

"An uppty nigger," said the white loafers when they saw him standing, slim and elegant, on the station platform in the September sunlight, surrounded by his bags with the bright stickers. Roy had got off a Pullman—something unusual for a Negro in those parts.

"God damn!" said the white loafers.

Suddenly a nasal voice broke out, "Well, I'll be dogged if it ain't Roy Williams!"

Roy recognized an old playmate, Charlie Mumford, from across the alley—a tall red-necked white boy in overalls. He took off his glove and held out his hand. The white man took it, but he didn't shake it long. Roy had forgotten he wasn't in Europe, wearing gloves and shaking hands glibly with a white man! Damn!

"Where you been, boy?" the white fellow asked.

"Paris," said Roy.

"What'd yuh come back for?" a half-southern voice drawled from the edge of a baggage truck.

"I wanted to come home," said Roy, "to see my mother."

"I hope she's gladder to see yuh than we are," another white voice drawled.

Roy picked up his bags, since there were no por-
ters, and carried them toward a rusty old Ford that
seemed to be a taxi. He felt dizzy and weak. The
smoke and dust of travel had made him cough a lot.
The eyes of the white men about the station were
not kind. He heard some one mutter, "Nigger."
His skin burned. For the first time in half a dozen
years he felt his color. He was home.

III

Sing a song of Dixie, cotton bursting in the sun,
shade of chinaberry trees, persimmons after frost
has fallen. Hounds treeing possums October nights.
O, sweet potatoes, hot, with butter in their yellow
hearts.

"Son, I'm glad you's done come home. What can
Ma cook for you? I know you's hungry for some
real food. Corn bread and greens and salt pork.
Lawd! . . . You's got some mighty nice clothes,
honey, but you looks right thin. . . . Chile, I hope
you's gonna stay home awhile. . . . These colored
girls here'll go crazy about you. They fightin' over
you already. . . . Honey, when you plays that
violin o' your'n it makes me right weak, it's so
purty. . . . Play yo' violin, boy! God's done give
you a gift! Yes, indeedy! . . . It's funny how all
these Hopkinsville white folks is heard about you
already. De woman where yo' sister works say she

read someplace 'bout that orchestry you was playin'
with in Paris. She says fo' Sister to bring you up to
de house to play fo' her sometime. I told Sister, no
indeedy, you don't go around playin' at nobody's
house. Told her to tell that white woman de
Deacon's Board's arrangin' a concert at de church
fo' you where everybody can come and pay twenty-
five cents to de glory of God and hear you play.
Ain't that right, son? You gwine play fo' de Lawd
here in Hopkinsville. You been playin' fo' de devil
every night all over Europy. . . . Jesus have
mercy! Lemme go and get ma washin' out! And
whiles you's practicin', I'm gonna make you a
pumpkin pie this afternoon. I can see yo' mouth
a-waterin' now. . . . Honey, Ma's sho glad you's
done come home. . . . Play yo' violin, son!"

IV

CAPRICE VIENNOIS
AIR FOR G STRING
SONATA IN A
AVE MARIA
THE GYPSY DANCES

What little house anywhere was ever big enough
to hold Brahms and Beethoven, Bach and César
Franck? Certainly not Sister Sarah Williams's
house in Hopkinsville. When Roy played, ill as he
was, the notes went bursting out the windows and

the colored folks and white folks in the street heard them. The classic Mr. Brahms coming out of a nigger's house in the southern end of Missouri. O, my God! Play yo' violin, Roy! Tonight's your concert.

The Deacons and the Ladies' Aid sold a lot of tickets to the white folks they worked for. Roy's home-coming concert at Shiloh Church was a financial success. The front rows were fifty cents and filled with white folks. The rest of the seats were a quarter and filled with Negroes. Methodist and Baptist both came, forgetting churchly rivalry. And there were lots of colored girls with powdered bonbon faces—sweet black and brown and yellow girls with red mouths pointed at Roy. There was lots of bustle and perfume and smothered giggling and whispered talk as the drab little church filled. New shoes screeched up and down the aisles. People applauded because it was past the hour, but the concert started colored folks' time anyhow—late. The church was crowded.

v

Hello, Mr. Brahms on a violin from Vienna at a colored church in Hopkinsville, Missouri. The slender brown-skin hands of a sick young man making you sing for an audience of poor white folks and even poorer Negroes. Good-evenin', Mr. Brahms, a long ways from home, travellin' in answer to your dream, singin' across the world. I had a dream, too, Mr. Brahms, a big dream that can't come true, now. Dream of a great stage in a huge hall, like Carnegie Hall or the Salle Gaveau. And you, Mr. Brahms, singin' out into the darkness, singin' so strong and true that a thousand people look up at me like they do at Roland Hayes singing the Crucifixion. Jesus, I dreamed like that once before I got sick and had to come home.

And here I am giving my first concert in America for my mother and the Deacons of Shiloh Church and the quarters and fifty cent pieces they've collected from Brahms and me for the glory of God. This ain't Carnegie Hall. I've only just come home. . . . But they're looking at me. They're all looking at me. The white folks in the front rows and the Negroes in the back. Like one pair of eyes looking at me.

This, my friends . . . I should say, *Ladies and Gentlemen.* (There are white folks in the audience who are not my friends.) . . . This is the *Meditation from Thaïs* by Massenet. . . . This is the broken heart of a dream come true not true. This is music, and me, sitting on the door-step of the world needing you. . . . O, body of life and love with black hands and brown limbs and white breasts and a golden face with lips like a violin bowed for singing. . . . Steady, Roy! It's hot in this crowded church, and you're sick as hell. . . . This, the

dream and the dreamer, wandering in the desert
from Hopkinsville to Vienna in love with a street-
walker named Music. . . . Listen, you bitch, I
want you to be beautiful as the moon in the night
on the edge of the Missouri hills. I'll make you
beautiful. . . . The *Meditation from Thaïs*. . . .
You remember, Ma (even to hear me play, you've
got your seat in the amen corner tonight like on
Sunday mornings when you come to talk to God),
you remember that Kreisler record we had on the
phonograph with the big horn when I was a kid?
Nobody liked it but me, but you didn't care how
many times I played it, over and over. . . .
Where'd you get my violin? Half the time you
didn't have the money to pay old man Miller for
my lesson every week. . . . God rest his unpaid
soul, as the Catholics say. . . . Why did you cry,
Ma, when I went away with the minstrel show, playing coon songs through the South instead of hymns?
What did you cry for, Ma, when I wrote you I had
a job with a night-club jazz band on State Street in
Chicago? . . . Why did you pray all night when I
told you we had a contract to go to Berlin and work
in a cabaret there? I tried to explain to you that the
best violin teachers in the world were in Berlin and
that I'd come back playing like that Kreisler record
on the old victrola. . . . And didn't I send you
money home? . . . Spray like sand in the eyes.
. . . O, dream on the door-step of the world! Thaïs!

Thaïs! . . . You sure don't look like Thaïs, you
scrawny white woman in a cheap coat and red hat
staring up at me from the first row. You don't look
a bit like Thaïs. What is it you want the music to
give you? What do you want from me? . . . This
is Hopkinsville, Missouri. . . . Look at all those
brown girls back there in the crowd of Negroes,
leaning toward me and the music. First time most of
them ever saw a man in evening clothes, black or
white. First time most of them ever heard the *Meditation from Thaïs*. First time they ever had one of
their own race come home from abroad playing a
violin. See them looking proud at me and music
over the heads of the white folks in the first rows,
over the head of the white woman in the cheap coat
and red hat who knows what music's all about. . . .
Who are you, lady?

When the concert was over, even some of the
white folks shook Roy's hand and said it was wonderful. The colored folks said, "Boy, you sure can
play!" Roy was shaking a little and his eyes burned
and he wanted terribly to cough. Pain shot across
his shoulders. But he smiled his concert-jazz-band
smile that the gold spending ladies of the European
night clubs had liked so much. And he held out a
feverish hand to everybody. The white woman in
the red hat waited at the edge of the crowd.

When people thinned out a little from the pulpit,

she came to Roy and shook his hand. She spoke of symphony concerts in St. Louis, of the fact that she was a teacher of music, of piano and violin, but that she had no pupils like Roy, that never in the town of Hopkinsville had anyone else played so beautifully. Roy looked into her thin, freckled face and was glad she knew what it was all about. He was glad she liked music.

"That's Miss Reese," his mother told him after she had gone. "An old maid musicianer at the white high school."

"Yes'm," said Roy. "She understands music."

VI

The next time he saw Miss Reese was at the white high school shortly after it opened the fall session. One morning a note had come asking him if he would play for her Senior class in music appreciation some day. She would accompany him if he would bring his music. It seems that one of Miss Reese's duties was the raising of musical standards in Hopkinsville; she had been telling her students about Bach and Mozart, and she would so appreciate it if Roy would visit the school and play those two great masters for her young people. She wrote him a nice note on clean white paper.

Roy went. His mother thought it was a great honor for the white high school to send for her colored son to play for them. "That Miss Reese's a right nice woman," Sister Williams said to her boy. "Sendin' for you to play up there at de school. First time I ever knowed 'em to have a Negro in there for anything but cleanin' up, and I been in Hopkinsville a long time. Go and play for 'em, son, to de glory of God!"

Roy played. But it was one of those days when his throat was hot and dry, and his eyes burned. He had been coughing all morning and, as he played, his breath left him and he stood covered with a damp sweat. He played badly.

But Miss Reese was more than kind to him. She accompanied him at the piano. And when he had finished, she turned to the assembled class of white kids sprawled in their seats and said, "This is art, my dear young people, this is true art!"

The students went home that afternoon and told their parents that a dressed-up nigger had come to school with a violin and played a lot of funny pieces nobody but Miss Reese liked. They went on to say that Miss Reese had grinned all over herself and cried, "Wonderful!" And had even bowed to the nigger when he went out!

Roy went home to bed. He was up and down these days, thinner and thinner all the time, weaker and weaker. Sometimes not practicing any more. Often not eating the food his mother cooked for him, or that his sister brought from where she worked. Sometimes being restless and hot in the night and getting up and dressing, even to spats and yellow gloves, and walking the streets of the little town at ten and eleven o'clock after nearly every one else had gone to bed. Midnight was late in Hopkinsville. But for years Roy had worked at night. It was hard for him to sleep before morning now.

But one night he walked out of the house for the last time. The moon had risen and Roy scarcely needed to light the oil lamp to dress by when he got up. The moon shone into his little room, across the white counterpane of his bed, down onto the bags with the bright stickers piled against the wall. It glistened on the array of medicine bottles on the side table. But Roy lighted the light, the better to see himself in the warped mirror of the dresser. Ashy pale his face was, that had once been brown. His cheeks were sunken. Trembling, he put on his suit and spats and his yellow gloves and soft felt hat. He got into an overcoat. He took a cane that he carried lately from weakness rather than from style. And he went out into the autumn moonlight.

Tiptoeing through the parlor, he heard his mother snoring on the couch there. (She had given up her room to him.) The front door was still unlocked. His brothers, Roy thought, were out with their girl friends. His sister had gone to bed.

In the streets it was very quiet. Misty with moonlight, the trees stood half clad in autumn leaves.

Roy walked under the dry falling leaves toward the center of the town, breathing in the moonlight air and swinging his cane. Night and the streets always made him feel better. He remembered the boulevards of Paris and the Unter den Linden. He remembered Tauber singing *Wien, Du Stadt Meiner Traume.* His mind went back to the lights and the music of the cities of Europe. How like a dream that he had ever been in Europe at all, he thought. Ma never had any money. Her kids had barely managed to get through the grade school. There was no higher school for Negroes in Hopkinsville. For him there had been only a minstrel show to run away with for further education. Then that chance with a jazz band going to Berlin. And his violin for a mistress all the time—with the best teachers his earnings could pay for abroad. Jazz at night and the classics in the morning. Hard work and hard practice, until his violin sang like nobody's business. Music, real music! Then he began to cough in Berlin.

Roy was passing lots of people now in the brightness of the main street, but he saw none of them. He saw only dreams and memories, and heard music. Some of the people stopped to stare and grin at the flare of the European coat on his slender brown body. Spats and a cane on a young nigger in Hopkinsville, Missouri! What's the big idea, heh? A little white boy or two catcalled, "Hey, coon!"

But everything might have been all right, folks might only have laughed or commented and cussed, had not a rather faded woman in a cheap coat and a red hat, a white woman, stepping out of the drug store just as Roy passed, bowed pleasantly to him, "Good evening."

Roy started, bowed, nodded, "Good evening, Miss Reese," and was glad to see her. Forgetting he wasn't in Europe, he took off his hat and his gloves, and held out his hand to this lady who understood music. They smiled at each other, the sick young colored man and the aging music teacher in the light of the main street. Then she asked him if he was still working on the Sarasate.

"Yes," Roy said. "It's lovely."

"And have you heard that marvellous Heifetz record of it?" Miss Reese inquired.

Roy opened his mouth to reply when he saw the woman's face suddenly grow pale with horror. Before he could turn around to learn what her eyes had seen, he felt a fist like a ton of bricks strike his jaw. There was a flash of lightning in his brain as his head hit the edge of the plate glass window of the drug store. Miss Reese screamed. The sidewalk filled with white young ruffians with red-necks, open sweaters, and fists doubled up to strike. The movies had just let out and the crowd, passing by and seeing, objected to a Negro talking to a white woman—insulting a White Woman—attacking a

WHITE woman—RAPING A WHITE WOM-
AN. They saw Roy remove his gloves and bow.
When Miss Reese screamed after Roy had been
struck, they were sure he had been making love to
her. And before the story got beyond the rim of the
crowd, Roy had been trying to rape her, right there
on the main street in front of the brightly-lighted
windows of the drug store. Yes, he did, too! Yes, sir!

So they knocked Roy down. They trampled on
his hat and cane and gloves as a dozen men tried to
get to him to pick him up—so some one else could
have the pleasure of knocking him down again.
They struggled over the privilege of knocking him
down.

Roy looked up from the sidewalk at the white
mob around him. His mouth was full of blood and
his eyes burned. His clothes were dirty. He wondered why Miss Reese had stopped to ask him about
Sarasate. He knew he would never get home to his
mother now.

Some one jerked him to his feet. Some one spat
in his face. (It looked like his old playmate, Charlie
Mumford.) Somebody cussed him for being a nigger, and another kicked him from behind. And all
the men and boys in the lighted street began to yell
and scream like mad people, and to snarl like dogs,
and to pull at the little Negro in spats they were
dragging through the town towards the woods.

The little Negro whose name was Roy Williams

began to choke on the blood in his mouth. And the roar of their voices and the scuff of their feet were split by the moonlight into a thousand notes like a Beethoven sonata. And when the white folks left his brown body, stark naked, strung from a tree at the edge of town, it hung there all night, like a violin for the wind to play.

PASSING

Chicago,
Sunday, Oct. 10.

Dear Ma,

I felt like a dog, passing you downtown last night and not speaking to you. You were great, though. Didn't give a sign that you even knew me, let alone I was your son. If I hadn't had the girl with me, Ma, we might have talked. I'm not as scared as I used to be about somebody taking me for colored any more just because I'm seen talking on the street to a Negro. I guess in looks I'm sort of suspect-proof, anyway. You remember what a hard time I used to have in school trying to convince teachers I was really colored. Sometimes, even after they met you, my mother, they wouldn't believe it. They just thought I had a mulatto mammy, I guess. Since I've begun to pass for white, nobody has ever doubted that I am a white man. Where I work, the boss is a Southerner and is always cussing out Negroes in my presence, not dreaming I'm one. It is to laugh!

Funny thing, though, Ma, how some white people certainly don't like colored people, do they? (If
they did, then I wouldn't have to be passing to keep
my good job.) They go out of their way sometimes
to say bad things about colored folks, putting it out
that all of us are thieves and liars, or else diseased—
consumption and syphilis, and the like. No wonder
it's hard for a black man to get a good job with that
kind of false propaganda going around. I never
knew they made a practice of saying such terrible
things about us until I started passing and heard
their conversations and lived their life.

But I don't mind being "white", Ma, and it was
mighty generous of you to urge me to go ahead and
make use of my light skin and good hair. It got me
this job, Ma, where I still get $65 a week in spite of
the depression. And I'm in line for promotion to
the chief office secretary, if Mr. Weeks goes to Washington. When I look at the colored boy porter who
sweeps out the office, I think that that's what I
might be doing if I wasn't light-skinned enough to
get by. No matter how smart that boy'd get to be,
they wouldn't hire him for a clerk in the office, not
if they knew it. Only for a porter. That's why I
sometimes get a kick out of putting something over
on the boss, who never dreams he's got a colored
secretary.

But, Ma, I felt mighty bad about last night. The
first time we'd met in public that way. That's the

kind of thing that makes passing hard, having to deny your own family when you see them. Of course, I know you and I both realize it is all for the best, but anyhow it's terrible. I love you, Ma, and hate to do it, even if you say you don't mind.

But what did you think of the girl with me, Ma? She's the kid I'm going to marry. Pretty good look-ing, isn't she? Nice disposition. The parents are well fixed. Her folks are German-Americans and don't have much prejudice about them, either. I took her to see a colored revue last week and she thought it was great. She said, "Darkies are so graceful and gay." I wonder what she would have said if I'd told her *I* was colored, or half-colored—that my old man was white, but you weren't? But I guess I won't go into that. Since I've made up my mind to live in the white world, and have found my place in it (a good place), why think about race any more? I'm glad I don't have to, I know that much.

I hope Charlie and Gladys don't feel bad about me. It's funny I was the only one of the kids light enough to pass. Charlie's darker than you, even, Ma. I know he sort of resented it in school when the teachers used to take me for white, before they knew we were brothers. I used to feel bad about it, too, then. But now I'm glad you backed me up, and told me to go ahead and get all I could out of life. That's what I'm going to do, Ma. I'm going to marry white and live white, and if any of my kids are born dark I'll swear they aren't mine. I won't get caught in the mire of color again. Not me. I'm free, Ma, free!

I'd be glad, though, if I could get away from Chicago, transferred to the New York office, or the San Francisco branch of the firm—somewhere where what happened last night couldn't ever occur again. It was awful passing *you* and not speaking. And if Gladys or Charlie were to meet me in the street, they might not be as tactful as you were— because they don't seem to be very happy about my passing for white. I don't see why, though. I'm not hurting them any, and I send you money every week and help out just as much as they do, if not more. Tell them not to queer me, Ma, if they should ever run into me and the girl friend any place. Maybe it would have been better if you and they had stayed in Cincinnati and I'd come away alone when we decided to move after the old man died. Or at least, we should have gone to different towns, shouldn't we?

Gee, Ma, when I think of how papa left everything to his white family, and you couldn't legally do anything for us kids, my blood boils. You wouldn't have a chance in a Kentucky court, I know, but maybe if you'd tried anyway, his white children would have paid you something to shut up. Maybe they wouldn't want it known in the papers that they had colored brothers. But you was too proud, wasn't you, Ma? I wouldn't have been so proud.

Well, he did buy you a house and send all us kids through school. I'm glad I finished college in Pittsburgh before he died. It was too bad about Charlie and Glad having to drop out, but I hope Charlie gets something better to do than working in a garage. And from what you told me in your last letter about Gladys, I don't blame you for being worried about her—wanting to go in the chorus of one of those South Side cabarets. Lord! But I know it's really tough for girls to get any kind of a job during this depression, especially for colored girls, even if Gladys is high yellow, and smart. But I hope you can keep her home, and out of those South Side dumps. They're no place for a good girl.

Well, Ma, I will close because I promised to take my weakness to the movies this evening. Isn't she sweet to look at, all blonde and blue-eyed? We're making plans about our house when we get married. We're going to take a little apartment on the North Side, in a good neighborhood, out on one of those nice quiet side streets where there are trees. I will take a box at the Post Office for your mail. Anyhow, I'm glad there's nothing to stop letters from crossing the color-line. Even if we can't meet often, we can write, can't we, Ma?

With love from your son,

JACK.

V

A GOOD JOB GONE

IT WAS A GOOD JOB. Best job I ever had. Got it my last year in high school and it took me damn near through college. I'm sure sorry it didn't last. I made good money, too. Made so much I changed from City College to Columbia my Sophomore year. Mr. Lloyd saw to it I got a good education. He had nothing against the Negro race, he said, and I don't believe he did. He certainly treated me swell from the time I met him till that high brown I'm gonna tell you about drove him crazy.

Now, Mr. Lloyd was a man like this: he had plenty of money, he liked his licker, and he liked his women. That was all. A damn nice guy—till he got hold of this jane from Harlem. Or till she got hold of him. My people—they won't do. They'd mess up the Lord if He got too intimate with 'em. Poor Negroes! I guess I was to blame. I should of told Mr. Lloyd she didn't mean him no good. But I was minding my own business, and I minded it too well.

That was one of the things Mr. Lloyd told me when I went to work there. He said, "Boy, you're working for me—nobody else. Keep your mouth shut about what goes on here, and I'll look out for you. You're in school, ain't you? Well, you won't have to worry about money to buy books and take your friends out—if you stay with me."

He paid me twenty-two dollars a week, and I ate and slept in. He had a four room apartment, as cozy a place as you'd want to see, looking right over Riverside Drive. Swell view. In the summer when Mr. Lloyd was in Paris, I didn't have a damn thing to do but eat and sleep, and air the furniture. I got so tired that I went to summer school.

"What you gonna be, boy?" he said.

I said, "A dentist, I reckon."

He said, "Go to it. They make a hell of a lot of money—if they got enough sex appeal."

He was always talking about sex appeal and lovin'. He knew more dirty stories, Mr. Lloyd did! And he liked his women young and pretty. That's about all I'd do, spend my time cleaning up after some woman he'd have around, or makin' sandwiches and drinks in the evenings. When I did something extra, he'd throw me a fiver any time. I made oodles o' money. Hell of a fine guy, Mr. Lloyd, with his 40-11 pretty gals—right out of the Scandals or the back pages of Vanity Fair—sweet and willing.

His wife was paralyzed, so I guess he had to have a little outside fun. They lived together in White

Plains. But he had a suite in the Hotel Roosevelt, and a office down on Broad. He says, when I got the job, "Boy, no matter what you find out about me, where I live, or where I work, don't *you* connect up w˙ᵗh no place but here. No matter what happens on Riverside Drive, don't you take it no further."

"Yes, sir, Mr Lloyd," I said, I knew where my bread was buttered. So I never went near the office or saw any of his other help but the chauffeur—and him a Jap.

Only thing I didn't like about the job, he used to bring some awfully cheap women there sometimes—big timers, but cheap inside. They didn't know how to treat a servant. One of 'em used to nigger and darkie me around, till I got her told right quietly one time, and Mr. Lloyd backed me up.

The boss said, "This is no ordinary boy, Lucille. True, he's my servant, but I've got him in Columbia studying to be a dentist, and he's just as white inside as he is black. Treat him right, or I'll see why." And it wasn't long before this Lucille dame was gone, and he had a little Irish girl with blue eyes he treated mean as hell.

Another thing I didn't like, though. Sometimes I used to have to drink a lot with him. When there was no women around, and Mr. Lloyd would get one of his blue spells and start talking about his wife, and how she hadn't walked for eighteen years, just laying flat on her back, after about an hour of this, he'd want me to start drinking with him. And when he felt good from licker he'd start talking about women in general, and he'd ask me what they were like in Harlem. Then he'd tell me what they were like in Montreal, and Havana, and Honolulu. He'd even had Gypsy women in Spain, Mr. Lloyd.

Then he would drink and drink, and make me drink with him. And we'd both be so drunk I couldn't go to classes the next morning, and he wouldn't go to the office all day. About four o'clock he'd send me for some clam broth and an American Mercury, so he could sober up on Mencken. I'd give him an alcohol rub, then he'd go off to the Roosevelt and have dinner with the society folks he knew. I might not see him again for days. But he'd slip me a greenback usually.

"Boy, you'll never lose anything through sticking with me! Here," and it would be a fiver.

Sometimes I wouldn't see Mr. Lloyd for weeks. Then he'd show up late at night with a chippie, and I'd start making drinks and sandwiches and smoothing down the bed. Then there'd be a round o' women, six or eight different ones in a row, for days. And me working my hips off keeping 'em fed and lickered up. This would go on till he got tired, and had the blues again. Then he'd beat the hell out of one of 'em and send her off. Then we'd get drunk. When he sobered up he'd telephone for his chauffeur and drive to White Plains to see his old lady, or down to the hotel where he lived with a secretary. And that would be that.

He had so damn much money, Mr. Lloyd. I don't see where folks get so much cash. But I don't care so long as they're giving some of it to me. And if it hadn't been for this colored woman, boy, I'd still be sitting pretty.

I don't know where he got her. Out of one of the Harlem night clubs, I guess. They came bustin' in about four o'clock one morning. I heard a woman laughing in the living-room, and I knew it was a colored laugh—one of ours. So deep and pretty, it couldn't have been nothing else. I got up, of course, like I always did when I heard Mr. Lloyd come in. I broke some ice, and took 'em out some drinks.

Yep, she was colored, all right. One of those golden browns, like an Alabama moon. Swell looking kid. She had the old man standing on his ears. I never saw him looking so happy before. She kept him laughing till daylight, hugging and kissing. She had a hot line, that kid did, without seemin' serious. He fell for it. She hadn't worked in Harlem speakeasies for nothing. Jesus! She was like gin and vermouth mixed. You know!

We got on swell, too, that girl and I. "Hy, Pal," she said when she saw me bringing out the drinks. "If it ain't old Harlem, on the Drive."

She wasn't a bit hinkty like so many folks when they're light-complexioned and up in the money.

If she hadn't been the boss's girl, I'd have tried to make her myself. But she had a black boy friend— a number writer on 135th Street—so she didn't need me. She was in love with him. Used to call him up soon as the boss got in the elevator bound for the office.

"Can I use this phone?" she asked me that very morning.

"Sure, Madam," I answered.

"Call me Pauline," she said, "I ain't white." And we got on swell. I cooked her some bacon and eggs while she called up her sweetie. She told him she'd hooked a new butter and egg man with bucks.

Well, the days went on. Each time, the boss would show up with Pauline. It looked like blondes didn't have a break—a sugar-brown had crowded the white babies out. But it was good for Mr. Lloyd. He didn't have the blues. And he stopped asking me to drink with him, thank God!

He was crazy about this Pauline. Didn't want no other woman. She kept him laughing all the time. She used to sing him bad songs that didn't seem bad when she was singing them, only seemed funny and good natured. She was nice, that girl. A gorgeous thing to have around the house.

But she knew what it was all about. Don't think she didn't. "You've got to kid white folks along," she said to me. "When you're depending on 'em for a living, make 'em *think* you like it."

"You said it," I agreed.

And she really put the bee on Mr. Lloyd. He bought her everything she wanted, and was as faithful to her as a husband. Used to ask me when she wasn't there, what I thought she needed. I don't know what got into him, he loved her like a dog.

She used to spend two or three nights a week with him—and the others with her boy-friend in Harlem. It was a hell of a long time before Mr. Lloyd found out about this colored fellow. When he did, it was pure accident. He saw Pauline going into the movies with him at the Capitol one night—a tall black good-looking guy with a diamond on his finger. And it made the old man sore.

That same night Mr. Lloyd got a ring-side table at the Cabin Club in Harlem. When Pauline came dancing out in the two o'clock revue, he called her, and told her to come there. He looked mad. Funny, boy, but that rich white man was jealous of the colored guy he had seen her with. Mr. Lloyd, jealous of a jig! Wouldn't that freeze you?

They had a hell of a quarrel that morning when they came to the apartment. First time I ever heard them quarrel. Pauline told him finally he could go to hell. She told him, yes, she loved that black boy, that he was the only boy she loved in the wide world, the only man she wanted.

They were all drunk, because between words they would drink licker. I'd left two bottles of Haig

& Haig on the tray when I went to bed. I thought
Pauline was stupid, talking like that, but I guess
she was so drunk she didn't care.

"Yes, I love that colored boy," she hollered. "Yes,
I love him. You don't think you're buying my heart,
do you?"

And that hurt the boss. He'd always thought he
was a great lover, and that women liked him for
something else besides his money. (Because most of
them wanted his money, nobody ever told him he
wasn't so hot. His girls all swore they loved him,
even when he beat them. They all let *him* put *them*
out. They hung on till the last dollar.)

But that little yellow devil of a Pauline evidently
didn't care what she said. She began cussing the
boss. Then Mr. Lloyd slapped her. I could hear it
way back in my bedroom where I was sleeping, with
one eye open.

In a minute I heard a crash that brought me to
my feet. I ran out, through the kitchen, through the
living-room, and opened Mr. Lloyd's door. Pauline
had thrown one of the whisky bottles at him. They
were battling like hell in the middle of the floor.

"Get out of here, boy!" Mr. Lloyd panted. So I
got. But I stood outside the door in case I was
needed. A white man beating a Negro woman
wasn't so good. If she wanted help, I was there. But
Pauline was a pretty tough little scrapper herself.
It sounded like the boss was getting the worst of it.

Finally, the tussling stopped. It was so quiet in there I thought maybe one of them was knocked out, so I cracked the door to see. The boss was kneeling at Pauline's feet, his arms around her knees.

"My God, Pauline, I love you!" I heard him say. "I want you, child. Don't mind what I've done. Stay here with me. Stay, stay, stay."

"Lemme out of here!" said Pauline, kicking at Mr. Lloyd.

But the boss held her tighter. Then she grabbed the other whisky bottle and hit him on the head. Of course, he fell out. I got a basin of cold water and put him in bed with a cloth on his dome. Pauline took off all the rings and things he'd given her and threw them at him, lying there on the bed like a ghost.

"A white bastard!" she said. "Just because they pay you, they always think they own you. No white man's gonna own me. I laugh with 'em and they think I like 'em. Hell, I'm from Arkansas where the crackers lynch niggers in the streets. How could *I* like 'em?"

She put on her coat and hat and went away.

When the boss came to, he told me to call his chauffeur. I thought he was going to a doctor, because his head was bleeding. But the chauffeur told me later he spent the whole day driving around Harlem trying to find Pauline. He wanted to bring her back. But he never found her.

He had a lot of trouble with that head, too. Seems like a piece of glass or something stuck in it. I didn't see him again for eight weeks. When I did see him, he wasn't the same man. No, sir, boy, something had happened to Mr. Lloyd. He didn't seem quite right in the head. I guess Pauline dazed him for life, made a fool of him.

He drank more than ever and had me so high I didn't know B from Bull's Foot. He had his white women around again, but he'd got the idea from somewhere that he was the world's greatest lover, and that he didn't have to give them anything but himself—which wasn't so forty for them little Broadway gold diggers who wanted diamonds and greenbacks.

Women started to clearing out early when they discovered Mr. Lloyd had gone romantic—and cheap. There were scandals and fights and terrible goings on when the girls didn't get their presents and checks. But Mr. Lloyd just said, "To hell with them," and drank more than ever, and let the pretty girls go. He picked up women off the streets and then wouldn't pay them, cheap as they are. Late in the night he would start drinking and crying about Pauline. The sun would be rising over the Hudson before he'd stop his crazy carryings on —making me drink with him and listen to the nights he'd spent with Pauline.

"I loved her, boy! She thought I was trying to

buy her. Some black buck had to come along and cut me out. But I'm just as good a lover as that black boy any day."

And he would begin to boast about the women he could have—without money, too. (Wrong, of course.) But he sent me to Harlem to find Pauline.

I couldn't find her. She'd gone away with her boy-friend. Some said they went to Memphis. Some said Chicago. Some said Los Angeles. Anyway, she was gone—that kid who looked like an Alabama moon.

I told Mr. Lloyd she was gone, so we got drunk again. For more'n a week, he made no move to go to the office. I began to be worried, cutting so many classes, staying up all night to drink with the old man, and hanging around most of the day. But if I left him alone, he acted like a fool. I was scared. He'd take out women's pictures and beat 'em and stamp on 'em and then make love to 'em and tear 'em up. Wouldn't eat. Didn't want to see anybody.

Then, one night, I knew he was crazy—so it was all up. He grabs the door like it was a woman, and starts to kiss it. I couldn't make him stop pawing at the door, so I telephoned his chauffeur. The chauffeur calls up one of Mr. Lloyd's broker friends. And they take him to the hospital.

That was last April. They've had him in the sanatorium ever since. The apartment's closed. His stuff's in storage, and I have no more job than a snake's got hips. Anyway, I went through college on it, but I don't know how the hell I'll get to dental school. I just wrote Ma down in Atlanta and told her times was hard. There ain't many Mr. Lloyd's, you can bet your life on that.

The chauffeur told me yesterday he's crazy as a loon now. Sometimes he thinks he's a stud-horse chasing a mare. Sometimes he's a lion. Poor man, in a padded cell! He was a swell guy when he had his right mind. But a yellow woman sure did drive him crazy. For me, well, it's just a good job gone!

Say, boy, gimme a smoke, will you? I hate to talk about it.

VI

REJUVENATION THROUGH
JOY

MR. EUGENE LESCHE IN A MORNING COAT, handsome beyond words, stood on the platform of the main ballroom of the big hotel facing Central Park at 59th Street, New York. He stood there speaking in a deep smooth voice, with a slight drawl, to a thousand well dressed women and some two or three hundred men who packed the place. His subject was "Motion and Joy", the last of his series of six Friday morning lectures, each of which had to do with something and Joy.

As the hour of his last lecture approached, expensive chauffeured motors turned off Fifth Avenue, circled around from the Park, drew up at the 59th Street entrance, discharged women. In the elevators leading to the level of the hotel ballroom, delicate foreign perfumes on the breasts of befurred ladies scented the bronze cars.

"I've just heard of it this week. Everybody's talking about him. Did you hear him before?"

"My dear, I shall have heard all six. . . . He sent me an announcement."

"Oh, why didn't I . . . ?"

"He's marvellous!"

"I simply can't tell you . . . "

The great Lesche speaking.

As he spoke, a thousand pairs of feminine eyes gazed as one. The men gazed, too. Hundreds of ears heard, entranced: Relax and be happy. Let Lesche tell you how to live. Lesche knows. Look at Lesche in a morning coat, strong and handsome, right here before you. Listen!

At $2.50 a seat (How little for his message!) they listened.

"Joy," said the great Lesche, "what is life without joy? . . . And how can we find joy? Not through sitting still with our world of troubles on our minds; not through taking thought—too often only another phrase for brooding; not by the sedentary study of books or pamphlets, of philosophies and creeds, of ancient lore; not through listening to *me* lecture or listening to any other person lecture," this was the *last* talk of his series, "but only through motion, through joyous motion; through life in motion! Lift up your arms to the sun," said Lesche. "Lift them up now! Right now," appealing to his audience. "Up, up, up!"

A thousand pairs of female arms, and some few hundred men's, were lifted up with great rustle and movement, then and there, toward the sun. They

were really lifted up toward Lesche, because nobody knew quite where the sun was in the crowded
ballroom—besides all eyes were on Lesche.

"Splendid," the big black-haired young man on
the platform said, "beautiful and splendid! That's
what life is, a movement up!" He paused. "But not
always up. The trees point toward the sun, but they
also sway in the wind, joyous in the wind. . . .
Keep your hands skyward," said Lesche, "sway!
Everybody sway! To the left, to the right, like trees
in the wind, sway!" And the huge audience began,
at Lesche's command, to sway. "Feet on the floor,"
said Lesche, "sway!"

He stood, swaying, too.

"Now," said Lesche suddenly, "stop!" Try to
move your hips! . . . Ah, you cannot! Seated as
you are in chairs, you cannot! The life-center, the
balance-point, cannot move in a chair. That is one
of the great crimes of modern life, one of the mur-
ders of ourselves, we sit too much in chairs. We
need to stand up—no, not now my friends." Some
were already standing. "Not *just* when you are listening to *me*. I am speaking now of a way of life. We
need to *live* up, point ourselves at the sun, sway in
the wind of our rhythms, walk to an inner and outer
music, put our balance-points in motion. (Do you
not remember my talk on 'Music and Joy'?) Primitive man never sits in chairs. Look at the Indians!

Look at the Negroes! They know how to move from the feet up, from the head down. Their centers live. They walk, they stand, they dance to their drum beats, their earth rhythms. They squat, they kneel, they lie—but they never, in their natural states, *never* sit in chairs. They do not mood and brood. No! They live through motion, through movement, through music, through joy! (Remember my lecture, 'Negroes and Joy'?) Ladies, and gentlemen, I offer you today—rejuvenation through joy."

Lesche bowed and bowed as he left the platform. With the greatest of grace he returned to bow again to applause that was thunderous. To a ballroom that was full of well-dressed women and cultured men, he bowed and bowed. Black-haired and handsome beyond words, he bowed. The people were loath to let him go.

Lesche had learned to bow that way in the circus. He used to drive the roan horses in the Great Roman Chariot Races—but nobody in the big ballroom of the hotel knew that. The women thought surely (to judge from their acclaim) that he had come fullblown right out of heaven to bring them joy.

Lesche knew what they thought, too, for within a month after the closing of his series of Friday Morning Lectures, they all received, at their town addresses, most beautifully written personal notes

announcing the opening in Westchester of his
Colony of Joy for the rebuilding of the mind, the
body, and the soul.

Unfortunately, we did not hear Lesche's lecture
on "Negroes and Joy" (the third in the series) but
he said, in substance, that Negroes were the hap-
piest people on earth. He said that they alone really
knew the secret of rhythms and of movements. How
futile, he said, to study Delsarte in this age! Go instead, he said, to Cab Calloway, Brick Top's, and
Bill Robinson! Move to music, he said, to the gaily
primitive rhythms of the first man. Be Adam
again, be Eve. Be not afraid of life, which is a garden. Be all this not by turning back time, but
merely by living to the true rhythm of our own
age, to music as modern as today, yet old as life,
music that the primitive Negroes brought with
their drums from Africa to America—that music,
my friends, known to the vulgar as jazz, but which
is so much *more* than jazz that we know not how to
appreciate it; that music which is the Joy of Life.
His letter explained that these rhythms would
play a great part in leading those—who would come
—along the path to joy. And at Lesche's initial Westchester colony, the leader of the music would be
none other than the famous Happy Lane (*a primi-
tif de luxe*), direct from the Moon Club in Harlem, with the finest Negro band in America. To be

both smart and modern in approaching the body and soul, was Lesche's aim. And to bring gaiety to a lot of people who had known nothing more joyous than Gurdijieff was his avowed intention—for those who could pay for it.

For Lesche's proposed path to life was not any less costly than that of the now famous master's at Fontainebleau. Indeed, it was even slightly more expensive. A great many ladies (and gentlemen, too) who received Lesche's beautifully written letter gasped when they learned the size of the initial check they would have to draw in order to enter, as a resident member, his Colony of Joy.

Some gasped and did *not* pay (because they could not), and so their lives went on without Joy. Others gasped, and paid. And several (enough to insure entirely Lesche's first season) paid without even gasping. These last were mostly old residents of Park Avenue or the better section of Germantown, ladies who had already tried everything looking toward happiness—now they wanted to try Joy, especially since it involved so new and novel a course as Lesche proposed—including the gaiety of Harlem Negroes, of which most of them knew nothing except through the rather remote chatter of the younger set who had probably been to the Cotton Club.

So Lesche opened up his house on an old estate

in Westchester with a mansion and several cottages thereon that the crash let him lease for a little or nothing. (Or rather, Sol, his manager, did the leasing.) Instead of chairs, they bought African stools, low, narrow, and backless.

"I got the best decorator in town, too," said Sol, "to do it over primitive—modernistic—on a percentage of the profits, if there are any."

"It's got to be comfortable," said Lesche, "so people can relax after they get through enjoying themselves."

"It'll be," said Sol.

"We're admitting nobody west of Fifth Avenue," said Lesche.

"No Broadwayites," said Sol.

"Certainly not," said Lesche. "Only people with souls to save—and enough Harlemites to save 'em."

"Ha! Ha!" said Sol.

All the attendants were French—maids, butlers, and pages. Lesche's two assistants were a healthy and hard young woman, to whom he had once been married, a Hollywood Swede with Jean Harlow hair; and a young Yale man who hadn't graduated, but who read Ronald Firbank seriously, adored Louis Armstrong, worshipped Dwight Fisk, and had written Lesche's five hundred personal letters in a seven-lively-arts Gilbert Seldes style.

Sol, of course, handled the money, with a staff of secretaries, bookkeepers, and managers. And

Happy Lane's African band, two tap dancers, and a real blues singer were contracted to spread joy, and act as the primordial pulse beat of the house. In other words, they were to furnish the primitive.

Within a month after the Colony opened in mid-January, its resident guests numbered thirty-five. Applications were legion. The demand for places was very great. The price went up.

"It's unbelievable how many people with money are unhappy," said Sol.

"It's unbelievable how they need what we got," drawled Lesche.

The press agents wrote marvellous stories about Lesche; how he had long been in his youth at Del Monte a student of the occult, how he had turned from that to the primitive and, through Africa, had discovered the curative values of Negro jazz.

The truth was quite otherwise.

Lesche had first worked in a circus. He rode a Roman chariot in the finale. All the way across the U. S. A. he rode twice daily, from Indianapolis where he got the job to Los Angeles where he quit, because nobody knew him there, and he liked the swimming at Santa Monica—and because he soon found a softer job posing for the members of a modernistic art colony who were modeling and painting away under a most expensive teacher at a nearby resort, saving their souls through art

Lesche ate oranges and posed and swam all that

summer and met a lot of nice, rich, and slightly faded women. New kind of people for him. Cultured people. He met, among others, Mrs. Oscar Willis of New Haven, one of the members of this colony of art expression. Her husband owned a railroad. She was very unhappy. She was lonely in her soul—and her pictures expressed that loneliness. She invited Lesche to tea at her bungalow near the beach.

Lesche taught her to swim. After that she was less unhappy. She began a new study in the painting class. She painted a circle and called it her impression of Lesche. It was hard to get it just right, so she asked him to do some extra posing for her in the late afternoons. And she paid him very well.

But summers end. Seasonal art classes too, and Mrs. Willis went back East.

Lesche worked in the movies as an extra. He played football for football pictures. Played gigolos for society films. Played a sailor, a cave man, a cop. He studied tap dancing. He did pretty well as far as earning money went, had lots of time for cocktails, parties, and books. Met lots of women.

He liked to read. He'd been a bright boy in high school back home in South Bend. And now at teas out Wilshire way he learned what one ought to read, and what one ought to have read. He spent money on books. Women spent money on him. He swam enough to keep a good body. Drank enough to be a good fellow, and acted well enough to have a job at the studios occasionally. He got married twice, but the other women were jealous, so divorces followed.

Then his friend Sol Blum had an idea. Sol ran a gym for the Hollywood elite. He had a newly opened swimming pool that wasn't doing so well. He asked Lesche if he would take charge of the lessons.

"Don't hurt yourself working, you know. Just swim around a little and show 'em that it looks easy. And be nice to the women," Sol said.

The swimming courses boomed. The fees went up. Sol and Lesche made money. (Lesche got a percentage cut.) He swam more and drank less. His body was swell, even if licker and women, parties and studio lights had made his face a little hard.

"But he's so damn nice," the women would say—who took swimming lessons for no good reason but to be held up by the black-haired Lesche.

Then one summer Lesche and Sol closed the gym and went to Paris. They drank an awful lot of licker at Harry's bar. And at Bricktop's they met an American woman who was giving a farewell party. She was Mrs. Oscar Willis, the artist—again—a long way from California.

"What's the idea?" said Lesche. "Are you committing suicide, Mrs. Willis, or going home, or what? Why a farewell party?"

"I am retiring from life," said Mrs. Willis, shouting above the frenzy of the Negro band. "I'm giving up art. I'm going to look for happiness. I'm going into the colony near Digne."

"Whose colony?" said Lesche. He remembered how much colonies cost, thinking of the art group.

"Mogador Bonatz's colony," said Mrs. Willis. "He's a very great Slav who can do so much for the soul. (Art does nothing.) Only one must agree to stay there six months when one goes."

"Is it expensive?" Lesche asked delicately. "I'm feeling awfully tired, too."

"Only $30 a day," said Mrs. Willis. "Have a drink?"

They drank a lot of champagne and said farewell to Mrs. Willis while the jazz band boomed and Bricktop shouted an occasional blues. Then Sol had an idea. After all, he was tired of gyms—why not start a colony? He mentioned it to Lesche when they got out into the open air.

"Hell, yes," said Lesche as they crossed Pigalle. "Let's start a colony."

From then on in Paris, Sol and Lesche studied soul cults. By night they went to Montmartre. By day they read occult books and thought how much people needed to retire and find beauty—and pay for it. By night they danced to the Negro jazz bands. And all the time they thought how greatly they needed a colony.

"You see how much people pay that guy Bonatz?" said Sol.

"Um-huh!" said Lesche, drinking from a tall glass at Josephine's. "And you see how much they'll spend on Harlem jazz, even in Paris?"

"Yeah," said Sol, "we're spending it ourselves. But what's that got to do with colonies?"

"Looks like to me," said Lesche, "a sure way to make money would be, combine a jazz band and a soul colony, and let it roll from there—black rhythm and happy souls."

"I see," said Sol. "That's not as silly as it sounds."

"Let 'em be mystic and have fun, too," said Lesche.

"What do you mean, mystic?" asked Sol.

"High brow fun," said Lesche. "Like they get from Bonatz. What do you suppose he's got we can't get?"

"Nothing," said Sol, who learned to sell ideas in Hollywood. "Now, you got the personality. With me for manager, a jazz band for background, and a little showmanship, it could be a riot."

"A riot is right," said Lesche.

When they returned to America, they stayed in New York. Sol got hold of a secretary who knew a lot of rich addresses and some rich people. Together they got hold of a smart young man from Yale who prepared a program of action for a high brow cult of joy—featuring the primitive. Then they got ready to open a Colony.

They cabled Mrs. Willis at Digne for the names of some of her friends who might need their souls fixed up—in America. They sent out a little folder. And they had the young Yale man write a few articles on *Contentment and Aboriginal Rhythms* for Lesche to try on the high brow magazines.

They really had a lot of nerve.

Lesche learned his lectures by heart that the college boy wrote. Then, he improvised, added variations of his own, made them personal, and bought a morning coat. Nightly he went to Harlem, brushing up on the newer rhythms. In November, they opened cold in the grand ballroom of the hotel facing the Park, without even a try-out elsewhere: Six lectures by Eugene Lesche on Joy in Relation to the Mind, Body, and Soul.

"Might as well take a big chance," said Sol. "Win or lose."

They won. In Sol's language, they wowed 'em. When the Friday Morning Series began, the ballroom was half full. When it ended, it was crowded and Sol had already signed the lease for the old Westchester estate.

So many people were in need of rejuvenating their souls and could seemingly still afford to pay for it that Sol gave up the idea for returning immediately to his gym in Hollywood. Souls seemed more important than bodies.

"How about it, Lesche?"

The intelligentsia dubbed their highly publicized efforts neo-paganism; others called it one more return to the primitive; others said out loud, it was a gyp game. Some said the world was turning passionate and spiritual; some said it was merely a sign of the decadence of the times. But everybody talked about it. The papers began to write about it. And the magazines that winter, from the *Junior League Bulletin* to the *Nation*, even the *New Masses*, remarked—usually snootily—but nevertheless remarked—about this Cult of Joy. (Harlem Hedonism, the *Forum* called it.) Lesche's publicity men who'd started it all, demanded higher wages, so Sol fired them. The thing went rolling of its own accord. The world was aware—of Joy! The Westchester Colony prospered.

Ten days before the January opening of the Colony, the huge mansion of the once aristocratic estate hummed with activity. It looked like a Broadway theatre before a première. Decorators were working for big effects. (They hoped *House And Garden*, *Vogue*, or *Vanity Fair* would picturize their super-modernistic results.) The house manager, a former hotel-head out of work, was busy getting his staff together—trying to keep them French—for the swank of it.

The bed-rooms were receiving special attention. At Lesche's, sleep also was to be a joy. And each private bathroom was being fitted with those special apparatus at colonies necessary for the cleansing of the body—for Sol and Lesche had hired a doctor to tell them what the best cults used.

"Body and soul," said Sol. "Body and soul."

"Gimme the body," said Lesche, "and let the Yale man take care of the soul."

Occult assistants, chefs and waitresses, *masseurs* and hairdressers, began to arrive—for the house was to be fully staffed. And there were plenty of first-class people out of work and willing to take a chance, too.

Upstairs in a third floor room, Lesche, like an actor preparing for a role, studied his lectures word for word. His former wife listened to him daily, reciting them by heart, puzzling over their allusions.

In another room, the Yale man, surrounded by books on primitive art, spiritual guidance, Negro jazz, German eurythmics, psychoanalysis, Yogi philosophy, all of Krishnamurti, half of Havelock Ellis, and most of Freud, besides piles of spirituals, jazz records, Paul Robeson, and Ethel Waters, and in the midst of all this—a typewriter. There sat the Yale man creating lectures—preparing, for a month in advance, twenty-minute daily talks for the great Lesche.

On the day when the Negroes arrived for their rehearsals, just prior to the opening of the place, Sol gave them a lecture. "Fellows," he said, addressing the band, "and Miss Lucas," to the blues-singing little coal-black dancer, "listen! Now I want to tell you about this place. This will not be no night club. Nor will it be a dance hall. This place is more like a church. It's for the rebuilding of souls—and bodies. It's for helping people. People who are wore out and tired, sick and bored, *ennui-ed* in other words, will come here for treatments, the kind of treatments, that Mr. Lesche and I have devised, which includes music, the best music, jazz, real primitive jazz out of Africa (you know, Harlem) to help 'em learn to move, to walk, to live in harmony with their times and themselves. Now, I want you all to be ladies and gentlemen (I know you are), to play with abandon, to give 'em all you got, but don't treat this like a rough house, nor like the Moon Club either. We allow only champagne drinkers here, cultured ladies, nice gentlemen, the best, the very best. Park Avenue. You know what I mean. . . . Now this is the order of the day. In the morning at eleven, Mr. Lesche will lecture in the Palm Garden, glass-enclosed, on the Art of

Motion and Rhythm. You, Miss Tulane Lucas, and you two tap dancers there, will illustrate. You will show grace in modern movements, aliveness, the beat of Africa as expressed through the body. Mr. Lesche will illustrate, too. He's one of Bill Robinson's disciples, you know! You all know how tap-dancing has preserved Bill. A man of his age, past fifty! Well, we want to show our clients how it can preserve them. But don't do no stunts now, just easy rhythm stuff. We got to start 'em off slow. Some of 'em is old. And I expect some is Christian Scientists. . . . Then in the late afternoon, we will have tea-dancing, just for pleasure. We want to give 'em plenty of exercise, so they won't be bored. And so they will eat. We expect to make money on our table, and on massages, too. In the evening for one hour, put on the best show you got, singing and dancing—every week we gonna bring up new specialities—send 'em to bed feeling happy, before Mr. Lesche gives his goodnight and sweet dreams talk. . . . Now, you boys understand, you'll be off early here, by ten or eleven. Not like at the Club. You got your own cottage here on the estate to live in, you got your cars. Don't mind you driving to town, if you want to, but I want you back here for the eleven o'clock services in the morning. And I don't want you sleepy, either. This house is dedicated to Joy, and all who work here have got to be bright and snappy. That's what our people are paying for.

. . . Lesche! Where is Lesche, Miss Boxall?"

The secretary looked startled. "He was in the halls talking to the new French maids."

"Well, get him in here. Tell him to explain to these boys how he wants to fix up his routine for his lectures. Let's get down to business now."

"What kind of clothes you want us to wear?" Happy Lane, the Negro leader, asked.

"Red," said Sol. "Red is the color of Joy."

"Lord!" said the blues singer, "I'm too dark to wear red!"

"That's what we want," said Sol, "darkness and light! We want to show 'em how much light there is in darkness."

"Now, here!" said the blues singer to herself, "I don't like no white folks talkin' 'bout me being dark."

"Lesche," Sol called to his partner strolling in through the door, "let's get going."

"O. K.," Lesche said. "Where's my boy?" meaning the Yale man.

"Right here, Gene."

"Now, how does that first lecture go?"

"My Gawd!" said Sol.

The Yale man referred to his notes. *"Joy,"* he read, *"Joy, springing from the dark rhythm of the primitive. . . ."*

"Oh, yes," said Lesche, turning to the band. "Now for that, give me *Mood Indigo,* you know, soft and syncopated, moan it soft and low. Then you, Miss Lucas," to the dancer, "you come gliding on. Give it plenty hip movement. I want 'em to learn to use their life-center. Then I'm gonna say . . . what's that boy-friend?" to the Yale man.

"*See how the . . .*"

"Oh, yes . . . *See how the Negroes live, dark as the earth, the primitive earth, swaying like trees, rooted in the deepest source of life.* . . . Then I'm gonna have 'em all rise and sway, like Miss Lucas here. . . . That ought to keep 'em from being bored until lunch time."

"Lawd," said Miss Lucas, muttering to herself, "what is this, a dancing school or a Sunday school?" And louder, "All right, Mr. Lesche, sounds like it might be a good act."

"Act, nothing," said Sol. "This is the art of life."

"Must be, if you say so," said Miss Lucas.

"Well, let's go," commanded the great Lesche. "Let's rehearse this first lecture now. Come on, boys."

The jazz band began to cry *Mood Indigo* in the best manner of the immortal Duke Ellington. Lesche began to speak in his great soft voice. Bushy-haired Tulane Lucas began to glide across the floor.

"Goddamn!" said Sol, "It's worth the money!"

"Hey! Hey!" said Miss Lucas.

"Sh-ss-ss-s!" said Lesche. "Be dignified . . .

rooted in the deepest source of life . . . er-r-r?"

". . . *O, early soul in motion . . .*" prompted the Yale man.

"*O, early soul . . .*" intoned Lesche.

The amazing collection of people gathered together in the Colony of Joy astounded even Lesche, whose very blasé-ness was what really made him appear so fresh. His thirty-seven clients in residence came almost all from families high in the Social Register, and equally high in the financial world. When Mrs. Carlos Gleed's check of entrance came in, Sol said, "Boy, we're made " . . . for of society there could be no higher—blue blood straight out of Back Bay.

The opening of the Colony created a furor among all the smart neurasthenics from Park Avenue right on up to New England. Dozens applied too late, and failed to get in. Others drove up daily for the lectures.

Of those who came, some had belonged formerly to the self-denial cults; others to Gurdijief; others had been analyzed in Paris, Berlin, Vienna; had consulted Adler, Hirschfeld, Freud. Some had studied *under* famous Yogi. Others had been at Nyack. Now they had come to the Colony of Joy.

Up and down Park Avenue miraculous gossip flew.

Why, Mrs. Charles Duveen Althouse of Newport and Paris—feeling bad for years—is said to look

like a cherub since she's gone into the Colony. . . .
My dear, the famous Oriental fan-painter, Vankulmer Jones—he's *another* man these days. The
rhythms, he says, the rhythms have worked
wonders! And just the very presence of Lesche
. . . Nothing America has ever known—rumor
flew about the penthouses of the East River—nothing is equal to it. . . . The Baroness Langstrund
gasped in a letter to a talkative friend, "My God,
it's marvellous!"

Far better than Indian thought, Miss Joan
Reeves, the heiress of Meadow Brook, was said to
have said by her best friends. "The movement is
amazing."

Almost all of them had belonged to cults before—cults that had never satisfied. Some had even
been injured by them. To a cult that based the soul-
search on self-denial—deny what you like best,
have it around you all the time, but never touch it,
never—then you will be strong—Mrs. Duveen
Althouse had belonged. She denied chocolates for
a whole year; kept fresh candy sitting in each corner of her boudoir—resisted with all her soul—and
at the end of a year was a wreck.

Mr. Jones, the fan-painter, had belonged to a
group on Cape Cod that believed in change
through change: that is, whatever you want to be,
you can. And all the members, after they had paid
their fees, were told by the Mystic Master to change

their names to whatever they most wished to be, or whoever, past or present, they admired. Some, without much depth, chose Napoleon or Cleopatra. But others, Daphne or Zeus or Merry del Val. Mr. Jones chose Horse. He'd always wanted to be an animal, to possess their strength and calm, their vigor, their ways. But after a whole summer at the Cape he was even less of a horse than before. And greatly mosquito bitten.

Mrs. Ken Prather, II, a member of Lesche's group, had once spent months entire kneeling holding her big toes behind her, deep in contemplation. A most handsome Indian came once a week to her home on East 64th, for an enormous consideration, and gave her lessons in silence, and in positions of thought. But finally she just couldn't stand it any more.

Others of the Colony of Joy had been Scientists in their youth. Others had wandered, disappointed, the ways of spiritualism, never finding soul-mates; still others had gazed solemnly into crystals, but had seen nothing but darkness; now, they had come to Joy!

How did it happen that nobody before had ever offered them Rejuvenation through Joy? Why, that was what they had been looking for all these years! And who would have thought it might come through the amusing and delightful rhythms of Negroes?

Nobody but Lesche.

In the warm glass-enclosed Palm Garden that winter, where the cupid fountain had been replaced by an enlargement of an African plastic and where a jazz band played soft and low behind the hedges, they felt (those who were there by virtue of their check books) all a-tremble in the depths of their souls after they had done their African exercises looking at Lesche—those slow, slightly grotesque, center-swaying exercises that he and Tulane Lucas from the Moon Club had devised. When they had finished, the movement, the music, and Lesche's voice, made them feel all warm and close to the earth, and as though they never wanted to leave the Colony of Joy or to be away from their great leader again.

Of course, there were a few who left, but their places were soon filled by others more truly mystic in the primitive sense than those whose arteries had already hardened, and who somehow couldn't follow a modern path to happiness, or sit on African stools. Clarence Lochard, for one, with *his* spine, had needed actual medical treatment not to be found at the Colony of Joy. And Mrs. J. Northcliff Hill, in the seventies, was a little too old for even the simple exercises that led to center-swaying. But for the two or three who went away, four or five came. And the house was full of life and soul.

Every morning, *ensemble,* they lifted up their hands to the sun when the earth-drums rang out—and the sun was Lesche, standing right there.

Lesche was called the New Leader. The Negro bandmaster was known as Happy Man. The dancers were called the Primitives. The drummer was ritualized as Earth-Drummer. And the devotees were called New Men, New Women—for the Yale man had written in one of the lectures, *"and the age-old rhythm of the earth as expressed by the drums is also the ever new rhythm of life. And all you who walk to it, dance to it, live to it, are New Men and New Women. You shall call one another, not by the old names but only New Man, New Woman, New One, forgetting the past."*

They called Lesche, Dear New Leader.

"For," continued the gist of that particular lecture, *"newness, eternal renewal, is the source of all growth, all life, and as we grow from day to day here in this colony, we shall be ever new, ever joyous and new."*

"Gimme sweet jazz on that line," Lesche had instructed at rehearsals. So on the thrilling morning of that lecture, the saxophones and clarinets moaned so beautiful and low, the drum beats called behind the palms with such wistful syncopation, that everybody felt impelled to move a new way as Lesche said, "Let us rise this morning and do a new dance, the dance of our new selves." And thirty-nine life-centers began to sway with the greatest of confidence in the palm court, for by now many inhibitions had fallen away, and the first exercise had been learned perfectly.

Who knows how long all might have gone on splendidly with Lesche and Sol and their Colony of Joy had not a most unhappy monster entered in to plague them. "The monster that's in every man," wrote the Yale man later in his diary, "the monster of jealousy—came to break down joy."

For the various New Ones became jealous of Lesche.

"It's your fault," stormed Sol. "Your fault. I told you to treat 'em all the same. I told you if you had to walk in the snow by moonlight, walk with your used-to-be wife, and leave the rest of these ladies alone. You know how women are. I told you not to start that Private Hour in the afternoon. I knew it would make trouble, create jealousy."

For out of the Private Hour devoted to the problems of each New One once a fortnight, where Lesche never advised (he couldn't) but merely received alone in confidence their troubles for contemplation, out of this private hour erelong, howls, screams, and recriminations were heard to issue almost daily. And in late March, New Woman Althouse was known to have thrown an African mask at New Leader Lesche because he kept her waiting a whole hour overtime while he devoted his attentions to the Meadow Brook heiress, New Woman Reeves.

"My Gawd!" said Sol, "the house is buzzing with scandal—I heard it all from Vankulmer Jones."

"These damn women," said Lesche, "I got to get rid of some of these women."

"You can't," said Sol. "They've all paid."

"Well, I will," said Lesche, "I'm tired! Why even my divorced wife's in love with me again. Fire her, will you?"

"Don't be foolish," said Sol, "she's a good secretary."

"Well, I'm gonna quit," said Lesche.

"You can't," said Sol. "I got you under contract."

"Oh, yeah?" said Lesche. "Too much is enough! And sometimes enough is too much! I'm tired, I tell you."

So they fell out. But Lesche didn't quit. It might have been better if he had, for Spring that year was all too sudden and full of implications. The very earth seemed to moan with excess of joy. Life was just too much to bear alone. It needed to be shared, its beauty given to others, taken in return. Its eternal newness united.

To the Colony, Lesche was their Leader, their life. And they wanted him, each one, alone. In desperation, he abolished the Private Hour. But that didn't help any. Mrs. Duveen Althouse was desperately in love with him now. (She called him Pan.) Miss Joan Reeves could not turn her eyes away. (He was her god.) Mrs. Carlos Gleed insisted that he summer at her island place in Maine. Baroness Langstrund announced quite definitely she intended to marry him—whereupon Mrs. Althouse, who had thrown the mask, threatened, without ceremony, to ring at once the Baroness' neck. Several other New Ones stopped speaking to each other over Lesche. Even the men members were taking sides for or against Lesche, or against each other. That dear soul Vankulmer Jones said he simply couldn't stand it any more—and left.

In the city, the Broadway gossip columns got hold of it—this excitement over Joy—and began to wise-crack. Then suddenly a minister started a crusade against the doings of the rich at the Colony and the tabloids sent men up to get pictures. Blackmailers, scenting scandal, began to blackmail. The righteous and the racketeers both sprang into action. And violets bloomed in April.

Sol tore his hair. "We're ruined!"

"Who cares?" said Lesche, "let's go back to the Hollywood gym. We made plenty on this. And I've still got the Hispano Mrs. Hancock donated."

"But we could've made millions."

"We'll come back to it next year," said Lesche. "And get some fresh New Ones. I'm damn tired of these old ones." And so they bickered.

But the final fireworks were set off by Miss Tulane Lucas, the dusky female of the Primitives. They began over the Earth-Drummer, and really had nothing to do with the Colony. But fire, once started, often spreads beyond control.

The drummer belonged to Miss Lucas. But when Spring came, he got a bad habit of driving down to New York after work every night and not getting back till morning.

"Another woman," said Tulane to herself, "after all I've done." She warned him, but he paid her no mind.

One April morning, just in time to play for the eleven o'clock lecture, with Lesche already on the platform, the little colored drummer arrived late and, without even having gone by the cottage to greet Tulane—rushed into the palm court and took his place at the earth-drums.

"Oh, no!" said Tulane suddenly from among the palms while all the New Ones, contemplating on their African stools, started at the unwonted sound. "Oh, no, you don't," she said. "You have drummed for your last time." And she took a pistol from her bosom and shot.

Bang! . . . Bang! . . . Bang!

Screams rent the palm court. As the drummer fled, bang! a bullet hit somewhere near his life-center, but he kept on. Pandemonium broke out.

"My Gawd!" said Sol. "Somebody grab that

gun." But Mrs. Duveen Althouse beat him to it. From Tulane, she snatched the weapon for herself and approached the great Lesche.

"How right to shoot the one you love!" she cried, "How primitive, how just!" And she pointed the gun directly at their dear Leader.

Again shots rang out. One struck the brass curve of the bass horn, glanced upward toward the ceiling, and crashed through the glass of the sun court, showering slivers on everybody.

But by that time, Baroness Langstrund had thrown herself on Duveen Althouse. "Aw-oo!" she screamed. "You wretch, shooting the man I love." Her fingers sought the other's hair, her nails tore at her eyes. Meanwhile, Mrs. Carlos Gleed threw an African stool.

Mrs. Althouse fired once more—but Lesche had gone. The final bullet hit only the marble floor, flew upward through the piano, and sounded a futile chord.

By this time, Sol had grabbed the gun. The screams died. Somebody separated the two women. Little French maids came running with water for the fainting. Happy Lane emerged from behind the bass-viol, pale as an African ghost—but nobody knew where the rest of the jazz band had disappeared, nor Lesche either. They were long gone.

There was no lecture that morning. Indeed,

there were never any more lectures. That was the end of the Colony of Joy.

The newspapers laughed about it for weeks, published pictures and names of the wealthy inmates; the columnists wisecracked. It was all very terrible! As a final touch, one of the tabloids claimed to have discovered that the great Lesche was a Negro —passing for white!

VII

THE BLUES I'M PLAYING

OCEOLA JONES, PIANIST, studied under Philippe in Paris. Mrs. Dora Ellsworth paid her bills. The bills included a little apartment on the Left Bank and a grand piano. Twice a year Mrs. Ellsworth came over from New York and spent part of her time with Oceola in the little apartment. The rest of her time abroad she usually spent at Biarritz or Juan les Pins, where she would see the new canvases of Antonio Bas, young Spanish painter who also enjoyed the patronage of Mrs. Ellsworth. Bas and Oceola, the woman thought, both had genius. And whether they had genius or not, she loved them, and took good care of them.

Poor dear lady, she had no children of her own. Her husband was dead. And she had no interest in life now save art, and the young people who created art. She was very rich, and it gave her pleasure to share her richness with beauty. Except that she was sometimes confused as to where beauty lay—in the youngsters or in what they made, in the creators or the creation. Mrs. Ellsworth had been known to help charming young people who wrote terrible poems, blue-eyed young men who painted awful pictures. And she once turned down a garlic-smelling soprano-singing girl who, a few years later, had all the critics in New York at her feet. The girl was so sallow. And she really needed a bath, or at least a mouth wash, on the day when Mrs. Ellsworth went to hear her sing at an East Side settlement house. Mrs. Ellsworth had sent a small check and let it go at that—since, however, living to regret bitterly her lack of musical acumen in the face of garlic.

About Oceola, though, there had been no doubt. The Negro girl had been highly recommended to her by Ormond Hunter, the music critic, who often went to Harlem to hear the church concerts there, and had thus listened twice to Oceola's playing.

"A most amazing tone," he had told Mrs. Ellsworth, knowing her interest in the young and unusual. "A flare for the piano such as I have seldom encountered. All she needs is training—finish, polish, a repertoire."

"Where is she?" asked Mrs. Ellsworth at once. "I will hear her play."

By the hardest, Oceola was found. By the hardest, an appointment was made for her to come to East 63rd Street and play for Mrs. Ellsworth. Oceola had said she was busy every day. It seemed that she had pupils, rehearsed a church choir, and played almost nightly for colored house parties or dances. She made quite a good deal of money. She wasn't tremendously interested, it seemed, in going way downtown to play for some elderly lady she had never heard of, even if the request did come from the white critic, Ormond Hunter, via the pastor of the church whose choir she rehearsed, and to which Mr. Hunter's maid belonged.

It was finally arranged, however. And one afternoon, promptly on time, black Miss Oceola Jones rang the door bell of white Mrs. Dora Ellsworth's grey stone house just off Madison. A butler who actually wore brass buttons opened the door, and she was shown upstairs to the music room. (The butler had been warned of her coming.) Ormond Hunter was already there, and they shook hands. In a moment, Mrs. Ellsworth came in, a tall stately grey-haired lady in black with a scarf that sort of floated behind her. She was tremendously intrigued at meeting Oceola, never having had before amongst all her artists a black one. And she was greatly impressed that Ormond Hunter should have recommended the girl. She began right away, treating her as a protegee; that is, she began asking her a great many questions she would not dare ask anyone else at first meeting, except a protegee. She asked her how old she was and where her mother and father were and how she made her living and whose music she liked best to play and was she married and would she take one lump or two in her tea, with lemon or cream?

After tea, Oceola played. She played the Rachmaninoff *Prelude in C Sharp Minor*. She played from the Liszt *Études*. She played the *St. Louis Blues*. She played Ravel's *Pavanne pour une Enfante Défunte*. And then she said she had to go. She was playing that night for a dance in Brooklyn for the benefit of the Urban League.

Mrs. Ellsworth and Ormond Hunter breathed, "How lovely!"

Mrs. Ellsworth said, "I am quite overcome, my dear. You play so beautifully." She went on further to say, "You must let me help you. Who is your teacher?"

"I have none now," Oceola replied. "I teach pupils myself. Don't have time any more to study—nor money either."

"But you must have time," said Mrs. Ellsworth, "and money, also. Come back to see me on Tuesday. We will arrange it, my dear."

And when the girl had gone, she turned to Ormond Hunter for advice on piano teachers to instruct those who already had genius, and need only to be developed.

II

Then began one of the most interesting periods in Mrs. Ellsworth's whole experience in aiding the arts. The period of Oceola. For the Negro girl, as time went on, began to occupy a greater and greater place in Mrs. Ellsworth's interests, to take up more and more of her time, and to use up more and more of her money. Not that Oceola ever asked for money, but Mrs. Ellsworth herself seemed to keep thinking of so much more Oceola needed.

At first it was hard to get Oceola to need anything. Mrs. Ellsworth had the feeling that the girl mistrusted her generosity, and Oceola did—for she had never met anybody interested in pure art before. Just to be given things for *art's sake* seemed suspicious to Oceola.

That first Tuesday, when the colored girl came back at Mrs. Ellsworth's request, she answered the white woman's questions with a why-look in her eyes.

"Don't think I'm being personal, dear," said Mrs. Ellsworth, "but I must know your background in order to help you. Now, tell me . . ."

Oceola wondered why on earth the woman wanted to help her. However, since Mrs. Ellsworth seemed interested in her life's history, she brought it forth so as not to hinder the progress of the afternoon, for she wanted to get back to Harlem by six o'clock.

Born in Mobile in 1903. Yes, m'am, she was older than she looked. Papa had a band, that is her stepfather. Used to play for all the lodge turn-outs, picnics, dances, barbecues. You could get the best roast pig in the world in Mobile. Her mother used to play the organ in church, and when the deacons bought a piano after the big revival, her mama played that, too. Oceola played by ear for a long while until her mother taught her notes. Oceola played an organ, also, and a cornet.

"My, my," said Mrs. Ellsworth.

"Yes, m'am," said Oceola. She had played and practiced on lots of instruments in the South before her step-father died. She always went to band rehearsals with him.

"And where was your father, dear?" asked Mrs. Ellsworth.

"My step-father had the band," replied Oceola. Her mother left off playing in the church to go with him traveling in Billy Kersands' Minstrels. He had the biggest mouth in the world, Kersands did, and used to let Oceola put both her hands in it at a time and stretch it. Well, she and her mama and step-papa settled down in Houston. Sometimes her parents had jobs and sometimes they didn't. Often they were hungry, but Oceola went to school and had a regular piano-teacher, an old German woman, who gave her what technique she had today.

"A fine old teacher," said Oceola. "She used to teach me half the time for nothing. God bless her."

"Yes," said Mrs. Ellsworth. "She gave you an excellent foundation."

"Sure did. But my step-papa died, got cut, and after that Mama didn't have no more use for Houston so we moved to St. Louis. Mama got a job playing for the movies in a Market Street theater, and I played for a church choir, and saved some money and went to Wilberforce. Studied piano there, too. Played for all the college dances. Graduated. Came to New York and heard Rachmaninoff and was crazy about him. Then Mama died, so I'm keeping the little flat myself. One room is rented out."

"Is she nice?" asked Mrs. Ellsworth, "your roomer?"

"It's not a she," said Oceola. "He's a man. I hate women roomers."

"Oh!" said Mrs. Ellsworth. "I should think all roomers would be terrible."

"He's right nice," said Oceola. "Name's Pete Williams."

"What does he do?" asked Mrs. Ellsworth.

"A Pullman porter," replied Oceola, "but he's saving money to go to Med school. He's a smart fellow."

But it turned out later that he wasn't paying Oceola any rent.

That afternoon, when Mrs. Ellsworth announced that she had made her an appointment with one of the best piano teachers in New York, the black girl seemed pleased. She recognized the name. But how, she wondered, would she find time for study, with her pupils and her choir, and all. When Mrs. Ellsworth said that she would cover her *entire* living expenses, Oceola's eyes were full of that why-look, as though she didn't believe it.

"I have faith in your art, dear," said Mrs. Ellsworth, at parting. But to prove it quickly, she sat down that very evening and sent Oceola the first monthly check so that she would no longer have to take in pupils or drill choirs or play at house parties. And so Oceola would have faith in art, too.

That night Mrs. Ellsworth called up Ormond Hunter and told him what she had done. And she asked if Mr. Hunter's maid knew Oceola, and if she supposed that that man rooming with her were anything to her. Ormond Hunter said he would inquire.

Before going to bed, Mrs. Ellsworth told her housekeeper to order a book called "Nigger Heaven" on the morrow, and also anything else Brentano's had about Harlem. She made a mental note that she must go up there sometime, for she had never yet seen that dark section of New York; and now that she had a Negro protegee, she really ought to know something about it. Mrs. Ellsworth couldn't recall ever having known a single Negro before in her whole life, so she found Oceola fascinating. And just as black as she herself was white.

Mrs. Ellsworth began to think in bed about what gowns would look best on Oceola. Her protegee would have to be well-dressed. She wondered, too, what sort of a place the girl lived in. And who that man was who lived with her. She began to think that really Oceola ought to have a place to herself. It didn't seem quite respectable. . . .

When she woke up in the morning, she called her car and went by her dressmaker's. She asked the good woman what kind of colors looked well with black; not black fabrics, but a black skin.

"I have a little friend to fit out," she said.

"A *black* friend?" said the dressmaker.

"A black friend," said Mrs. Ellsworth.

III

Some days later Ormond Hunter reported on what his maid knew about Oceola. It seemed that the two belonged to the same church, and although the maid did not know Oceola very well, she knew what everybody said about her in the church. Yes, indeedy! Oceola were a right nice girl, for sure, but it certainly were a shame she were giving all her money to that man what stayed with her and what she was practically putting through college so he could be a doctor.

"Why," gasped Mrs. Ellsworth, "the poor child is being preyed upon."

"It seems to me so," said Ormond Hunter.

"I must get her out of Harlem," said Mrs. Ellsworth, "at once. I believe it's worse than China-town."

"She might be in a more artistic atmosphere," agreed Ormond Hunter. "And with her career launched, she probably won't want that man any-how."

"She won't need him," said Mrs. Ellsworth. "She will have her art."

But Mrs. Ellsworth decided that in order to in-crease the rapprochement between art and Oceola, something should be done now, at once. She asked the girl to come down to see her the next day, and when it was time to go home, the white woman said, "I have a half-hour before dinner. I'll drive you up. You know I've never been to Harlem."

"All right," said Oceola. "That's nice of you."

But she didn't suggest the white lady's coming in, when they drew up before a rather sad-looking apartment house in 134th Street. Mrs. Ellsworth had to ask could she come in.

"I live on the fifth floor," said Oceola, "and there isn't any elevator."

"It doesn't matter, dear," said the white woman, for she meant to see the inside of this girl's life, elevator or no elevator.

The apartment was just as she thought it would be. After all, she had read Thomas Burke on Lime-house. And here was just one more of those holes in the wall, even if it was five stories high. The windows looked down on slums. There were only four rooms, small as maids' rooms, all of them. An upright piano almost filled the parlor. Oceola slept in the dining-room. The roomer slept in the bedchamber beyond the kitchen.

"Where is he, darling?"

"He runs on the road all summer," said the girl. "He's in and out."

"But how do you breathe in here?" asked Mrs. Ellsworth. "It's so small. You must have more space for your soul, dear. And for a grand piano. Now, in the Village . . ."

"I do right well here," said Oceola.

"But in the Village where so many nice artists live we can get . . ."

"But I don't want to move yet. I promised my roomer he could stay till fall."

"Why till fall?"

"He's going to Meharry then."

"To marry?"

"Meharry, yes m'am. That's a colored Medicine school in Nashville."

"Colored? Is it good?"

"Well, it's cheap," said Oceola. "After he goes, I don't mind moving."

"But I wanted to see you settled before I go away for the summer."

"When you come back is all right. I can do till then."

"Art is long," reminded Mrs. Ellsworth, "and time is fleeting, my dear."

"Yes, m'am," said Oceola, "but I gets nervous if I start worrying about time."

So Mrs. Ellsworth went off to Bar Harbor for the season, and left the man with Oceola.

IV

That was some years ago. Eventually art and Mrs. Ellsworth triumphed. Oceola moved out of Harlem. She lived in Gay Street west of Washington Square where she met Genevieve Taggard, and Ernestine Evans, and two or three sculptors, and a cat-painter who was also a protegee of Mrs. Ellsworth. She spent her days practicing, playing for friends of her patron, going to concerts, and reading books about music. She no longer had pupils or rehearsed the choir, but she still loved to play for Harlem house parties—for nothing—now that she no longer needed the money, out of sheer love of jazz. This rather disturbed Mrs. Ellsworth, who still believed in art of the old school, portraits that really and truly looked like people, poems about nature, music that had soul in it, not syncopation. And she felt the dignity of art. Was it in keeping with genius, she wondered, for Oceola to have a studio full of white and colored people every Saturday night (some of them actually drinking gin *from bottles*) and dancing to the most tomtom—like music she had ever heard coming out of a grand piano? She wished she could lift Oceola up bodily and take her away from all that, for art's sake.

So in the spring, Mrs. Ellsworth organized week-ends in the up-state mountains where she had a little lodge and where Oceola could look from the high places at the stars, and fill her soul with the vastness of the eternal, and forget about jazz. Mrs. Ellsworth really began to hate jazz—especially on a grand piano.

If there were a lot of guests at the lodge, as there sometimes were, Mrs. Ellsworth might share the bed with Oceola. Then she would read aloud Ten-nyson or Browning before turning out the light, aware all the time of the electric strength of that brown-black body beside her, and of the deep drowsy voice asking what the poems were about. And then Mrs. Ellsworth would feel very motherly toward this dark girl whom she had taken under her wing on the wonderful road of art, to nurture and love until she became a great interpreter of the piano. At such times the elderly white woman was glad her late husband's money, so well invested, fur-nished her with a large surplus to devote to the needs of her protegees, especially to Oceola, the blackest—and most interesting of all.

Why the most interesting?

Mrs. Ellsworth didn't know, unless it was that

Oceola really was talented, terribly alive, and that she looked like nothing Mrs. Ellsworth had ever been near before. Such a rich velvet black, and such a hard young body! The teacher of the piano raved about her strength.

"She can stand a great career," the teacher said. "She has everything for it."

"Yes," agreed Mrs. Ellsworth, thinking, however, of the Pullman porter at Meharry, "but she must learn to sublimate her soul."

So for two years then, Oceola lived abroad at Mrs. Ellsworth's expense. She studied with Philippe, had the little apartment on the Left Bank, and learned about Debussy's African background. She met many black Algerian and French West Indian students, too, and listened to their interminable arguments ranging from Garvey to Picasso to Spengler to Jean Cocteau, and thought they all must be crazy. Why did they or anybody argue so much about life or art? Oceola merely lived—and loved it. Only the Marxian students seemed sound to her for they, at least, wanted people to have enough to eat. That was important, Oceola thought, remembering, as she did, her own sometimes hungry years. But the rest of the controversies, as far as she could fathom, were based on air.

Oceola hated most artists, too, and the word *art* in French or English. If you wanted to play the piano or paint pictures or write books, go ahead!

But why talk so much about it? Montparnasse was worse in that respect than the Village. And as for the cultured Negroes who were always saying art would break down color lines, art could save the race and prevent lynchings! "Bunk!" said Oceola. "My ma and pa were both artists when it came to making music, and the white folks ran them out of town for being dressed up in Alabama. And look at the Jews! Every other artist in the world's a Jew, and still folks hate them."

She thought of Mrs. Ellsworth (dear soul in New York), who never made uncomplimentary remarks about Negroes, but frequently did about Jews. Of little Menuhin she would say, for instance, "He's a *genius*—not a Jew," hating to admit his ancestry.

In Paris, Oceola especially loved the West Indian ball rooms where the black colonials danced the beguin. And she liked the entertainers at Bricktop's. Sometimes late at night there, Oceola would take the piano and beat out a blues for Brick and the assembled guests. In her playing of Negro folk music, Oceola never doctored it up, or filled it full of classical runs, or fancy falsities. In the blues she made the bass notes throb like tom-toms, the trebles cry like little flutes, so deep in the earth and so high in the sky that they understood everything. And when the night club crowd would get up and dance to her blues, and Bricktop would yell, "Hey! Hey!" Oceola felt as happy as if she were performing a

Chopin étude for the nicely gloved Oh's and Ah-ers in a Crillon salon.

Music, to Oceola, demanded movement and expression, dancing and living to go with it. She liked to teach, when she had the choir, the singing of those rhythmical Negro spirituals that possessed the power to pull colored folks out of their seats in the amen corner and make them prance and shout in the aisles for Jesus. She never liked those fashionable colored churches where shouting and movement were discouraged and looked down upon, and where New England hymns instead of spirituals were sung. Oceola's background was too well-grounded in Mobile, and Billy Kersands' Minstrels, and the Sanctified churches where religion was a joy, to stare mystically over the top of a grand piano like white folks and imagine that Beethoven had nothing to do with life, or that Schubert's love songs were only sublimations.

Whenever Mrs. Ellsworth came to Paris, she and Oceola spent hours listening to symphonies and string quartettes and pianists. Oceola enjoyed concerts, but seldom felt, like her patron, that she was floating on clouds of bliss. Mrs. Ellsworth insisted, however, that Oceola's spirit was too moved for words at such times—therefore she understood why the dear child kept quiet. Mrs. Ellsworth herself was often too moved for words, but never by pieces like Ravel's *Bolero* (which Oceola played on the phonograph as a dance record) or any of the compositions of *les Six*.

What Oceola really enjoyed most with Mrs. Ellsworth was not going to concerts, but going for trips on the little river boats in the Seine; or riding out to old chateaux in her patron's hired Renault; or to Versailles, and listening to the aging white lady talk about the romantic history of France, the wars and uprising, the loves and intrigues of princes and kings and queens, about guillotines and lace handkerchiefs, snuff boxes and daggers. For Mrs. Ellsworth had loved France as a girl, and had made a study of its life and lore. Once she used to sing simple little French songs rather well, too. And she always regretted that her husband never understood the lovely words—or even tried to understand them.

Oceola learned the accompaniments for all the songs Mrs. Ellsworth knew and sometimes they tried them over together. The middle-aged white woman loved to sing when the colored girl played, and she even tried spirituals. Often, when she stayed at the little Paris apartment, Oceola would go into the kitchen and cook something good for late supper, maybe an oyster soup, or fried apples and bacon. And sometimes Oceola had pigs' feet.

"There's nothing quite so good as a pig's foot," said Oceola, "after playing all day."

"Then you must have pigs' feet," agreed Mrs. Ellsworth.

And all this while Oceola's development at the piano blossomed into perfection. Her tone became a singing wonder and her interpretations warm and individual. She gave a concert in Paris, one in Brussels, and another in Berlin. She got the press notices all pianists crave. She had her picture in lots of European papers. And she came home to New York a year after the stock market crashed and nobody had any money—except folks like Mrs. Ellsworth who had so much it would be hard to ever lose it all.

Oceola's one time Pullman porter, now a coming doctor, was graduating from Meharry that spring. Mrs. Ellsworth saw her dark protegee go South to attend his graduation with tears in her eyes. She thought that by now music would be enough, after all those years under the best teachers, but alas, Oceola was not yet sublimated, even by Philippe. She wanted to see Pete.

Oceola returned North to prepare for her New York concert in the fall. She wrote Mrs. Ellsworth at Bar Harbor that her doctor boy-friend was putting in one more summer on the railroad, then in the autumn he would intern at Atlanta. And Oceola said that he had asked her to marry him. Lord, she was happy!

It was a long time before she heard from Mrs.

Ellsworth. When the letter same, it was full of long paragraphs about the beautiful music Oceola had within her power to give the world. Instead, she wanted to marry and be burdened with children! Oh, my dear, my dear!

Oceola, when she read it, thought she had done pretty well knowing Pete this long and not having children. But she wrote back that she didn't see why children and music couldn't go together. Anyway, during the present depression, it was pretty hard for a beginning artist like herself to book a concert tour—so she might just as well be married awhile. Pete, on his last run in from St. Louis, had suggested that they have the wedding Christmas in the South. "And he's impatient, at that. He needs me."

This time Mrs. Ellsworth didn't answer by letter at all. She was back in town in late September. In November, Oceola played at Town Hall. The critics were kind, but they didn't go wild. Mrs. Ellsworth swore it was because of Pete's influence on her protegee.

"But he was in Atlanta," Oceola said.

"His spirit was here," Mrs. Ellsworth insisted. "All the time you were playing on that stage, he was here, the monster! Taking you out of yourself, taking you away from the piano."

"Why, he wasn't," said Oceola. "He was watching an operation in Atlanta."

But from then on, things didn't go well between

her and her patron. The white lady grew distinctly cold when she received Oceola in her beautiful drawing room among the jade vases and amber cups worth thousands of dollars. When Oceola would have to wait there for Mrs. Ellsworth, she was afraid to move for fear she might knock something over— that would take ten years of a Harlemite's wages to replace, if broken.

Over the tea cups, the aging Mrs. Ellsworth did not talk any longer about the concert tour she had once thought she might finance for Oceola, if no recognized bureau took it up. Instead, she spoke of that something she believed Oceola's fingers had lost since her return from Europe. And she wondered why any one insisted on living in Harlem.

"I've been away from my own people so long," said the girl, "I want to live right in the middle of them again."

Why, Mrs. Ellsworth wondered farther, did Oceola, at her last concert in a Harlem church, not stick to the classical items listed on the program. Why did she insert one of her own variations on the spirituals, a syncopated variation from the Sanctified Church, that made an old colored lady rise up and cry out from her pew, "Glory to God this evenin'! Yes! Hallelujah! Whooo-oo!" right at the concert? Which seemed most undignified to Mrs. Ellsworth, and unworthy of the teachings of Philippe. And furthermore, why was Pete coming up to New York for Thanksgiving? And who had sent him the money to come?

"Me," said Oceola. "He doesn't make anything interning."

"Well," said Mrs. Ellsworth, "I don't think much of him." But Oceola didn't seem to care what Mrs. Ellsworth thought, for she made no defense.

Thanksgiving evening, in bed, together in a Harlem apartment, Pete and Oceola talked about their wedding to come. They would have a big one in a church with lots of music. And Pete would give her a ring. And she would have on a white dress, light and fluffy, not silk. "I hate silk," she said. "I hate expensive things." (She thought of her mother being buried in a cotton dress, for they were all broke when she died. Mother would have been glad about her marriage.) "Pete," Oceola said, hugging him in the dark, "let's live in Atlanta, where there are lots of colored people, like us."

"What about Mrs. Ellsworth?" Pete asked. "She coming down to Atlanta for our wedding?"

"I don't know," said Oceola.

"I hope not, 'cause if she stops at one of them big hotels. I won't have you going to the back door to see her. That's one thing I hate about the South—where there're white people, you have to go to the back door."

"Maybe she can stay with us," said Oceola. "I wouldn't mind."

"I'll be damned," said Pete. "You want to get lynched?"

But it happened that Mrs. Ellsworth didn't care to attend the wedding, anyway. When she saw how love had triumphed over art, she decided she could no longer influence Oceola's life. The period of Oceola was over. She would send checks, occasionally, if the girl needed them, besides, of course, something beautiful for the wedding, but that would be all. These things she told her the week after Thanksgiving.

"And Oceola, my dear, I've decided to spend the whole winter in Europe. I sail on December eighteenth. Christmas—while you are marrying—I shall be in Paris with my precious Antonio Bas. In January, he has an exhibition of oils in Madrid. And in the spring, a new young poet is coming over whom I want to visit Florence, to really know Florence. A charming white-haired boy from Omaha whose soul has been crushed in the West. I want to try to help him. He, my dear, is one of the few people who live for their art—and nothing else. . . . Ah, such a beautiful life! . . . You will come and play for me once before I sail?"

"Yes, Mrs. Ellsworth," said Oceola, genuinely sorry that the end had come. Why did white folks think you could live on nothing but art? Strange! Too strange! Too strange!

v

The Persian vases in the music room were filled
with long-stemmed lilies that night when Oceola
Jones came down from Harlem for the last time to
play for Mrs. Dora Ellsworth. Mrs. Ellsworth had
on a gown of black velvet, and a collar of pearls
about her neck. She was very kind and gentle to
Oceola, as one would be to a child who has done a
great wrong but doesn't know any better. But to
the black girl from Harlem, she looked very cold
and white, and her grand piano seemed like the
biggest and heaviest in the world—as Oceola sat
down to play it with the technique for which Mrs.
Ellsworth had paid.

As the rich and aging white woman listened to
the great roll of Beethoven sonatas and to the sea
and moonlight of the Chopin nocturnes, as she
watched the swaying dark strong shoulders of Oceola Jones, she began to reproach the girl aloud for
running away from art and music, for burying herself in Atlanta and love—love for a man unworthy
of lacing up her boot straps, as Mrs. Ellsworth put
it.

"You could shake the stars with your music,
Oceola. Depression or no depression, I could make
you great. And yet you propose to dig a grave for
yourself. Art is bigger than love."

"I believe you, Mrs. Ellsworth," said Oceola, not turning away from the piano. "But being married won't keep me from making tours, or being an artist."

"Yes, it will," said Mrs. Ellsworth. "He'll take all the music out of you."

"No, he won't," said Oceola.

"You don't know, child," said Mrs. Ellsworth, "what men are like."

"Yes, I do," said Oceola simply. And her fingers began to wander slowly up and down the keyboard, flowing into the soft and lazy syncopation of a Negro blues, a blues that deepened and grew into rollicking jazz, then into an earth-throbbing rhythm that shook the lilies in the Persian vases of Mrs. Ellsworth's music room. Louder than the voice of the white woman who cried that Oceola was deserting beauty, deserting her real self, deserting her hope in life, the flood of wild syncopation filled the house, then sank into the slow and singing blues with which it had begun.

The girl at the piano heard the white woman saying, "Is this what I spent thousands of dollars to teach you?"

"No," said Oceola simply. "This is mine. . . . Listen! . . . How sad and gay it is. Blue and happy —laughing and crying. . . . How white like you and black like me. . . . How much like a man. . . . And how like a woman. . . . Warm as Pete's

mouth. . . . These are the blues. . . . I'm playing."

Mrs. Ellsworth sat very still in her chair looking
at the lilies trembling delicately in the priceless
Persian vases, while Oceola made the bass notes
throb like tomtoms deep in the earth.

> *O, if I could holler*

sang the blues,

> *Like a mountain jack,*
> *I'd go up on de mountain*

sang the blues,

> *And call my baby back.*

"And I," said Mrs. Ellsworth rising from her
chair, "would stand looking at the stars."

VIII

RED-HEADED BABY

"DEAD, DEAD AS HELL, these little burgs on the Florida coast. Lot of half-built skeleton houses left over from the boom. Never finished. Never will be finished. Mosquitoes, sand, niggers. Christ, I ought to break away from it. Stuck five years on same boat and still nothin' but a third mate puttin' in at dumps like this on a damned coast-wise tramp. Not even a good time to be had. Norfolk, Savannah, Jacksonville, ain't bad. Ain't bad. But what the hell kind of port's this? What the hell is there to do except get drunk and go out and sleep with niggers? Hell!"

Feet in the sand. Head under palms, magnolias, stars. Lights and the kid-cries of a sleepy town. Mosquitoes to slap at with hairy freckled hands and a dead hot breeze, when there is any breeze.

"What the hell am I walkin' way out here for? She wasn't nothin' to get excited over—last time I saw her. And that must a been a full three years ago. She acted like she was a virgin then. Name was Betsy. Sure ain't a virgin now, I know that. Not after we'd been anchored here damn near a month, the old man mixed up in some kind of law suit over some rich guy's yacht we rammed in a midnight squall off the bar. Damn good thing I wasn't on the bridge then. And this damn yellow gal, said she never had nothing to do with a seaman before. Lyin' I guess. Three years ago. She's probably on the crib-line now. Hell, how far was that house?"

Crossing the railroad track at the edge of town. Green lights. Sand in the road, seeping into oxfords and the cuffs of dungarees. Surf sounds, mosquito sounds, nigger-cries in the night. No street lights out here. There never is where niggers live. Rickety run-down huts, under palm trees. Flowers and vines all over. Always growing, always climbing. Never finished. Never will be finished climbing, growing. Hell of a lot of stars these Florida nights.

"Say, this ought to be the house. No light in it. Well, I remember this half-fallin'-down gate. Still fallin' down. Hell, why don't it go on and fall? Two or three years, and ain't fell yet. Guess *she's* fell a hell of a lot, though. It don't take them yellow janes long to get old and ugly. Said she was seventeen then. A wonder her old woman let me come in the house that night. They acted like it was the first time a white man had ever come in the house. They acted scared. But she was worth the money that time all right. She played like a kid. Said she liked my red hair. Said she'd never had a white man before. . . . Holy Jesus, the yellow wenches I've had, though. . . . Well, it's the same old gate. Be funny if she had another mule in my stall, now wouldn't it? . . . Say, anybody home there?"

"Yes, suh! Yes, suh! Come right in!"

"Hell, I know they can't recognize my voice. . . . It's the old woman, sure as a yard arm's long. . . . Hello! Where's Betsy?"

"Yes, suh, right here, suh. In de kitchen. Wait till I lights de light. Come in. Come in, young gentleman."

"Hell, I can't see to come in."

Little flare of oil light.

"Howdy! Howdy do, suh! Howdy, if 'tain't Mister Clarence, now, 'pon my word! Howdy, Mister Clarence, howdy! Howdy! After sich a long time."

"You must-a knowed my voice."

"No, suh, ain't recollected, suh. No, suh, but I knowed you was some white man comin' up de walk. Yes, indeedy! Set down, set down. Betsy be here directly. Set *right* down. Lemme call her. She's in de kitchen. . . . You Betsy!"

"Same old woman, wrinkled as hell, and still don't care where the money comes from. Still talkin' loud. . . . She knew it was some white man comin' up the walk, heh? There must be plenty of 'em, then, comin' here now. She knew it was some white man, heh! . . . What yuh sayin', Betsy, old gal? Damn if yuh ain't just as plump as ever. Them same damn moles on your cheek! Com'ere, lemme feel 'em."

Young yellow girl in a white house dress. Oiled hair. Skin like an autumn moon. Gold-ripe young yellow girl with a white house dress to her knees. Soft plump bare legs, color of the moon. Barefooted.

"Say, Betsy, here is Mister Clarence come back."

"Sure is! Claren—Mister Clarence! Ma, give him a drink."

"Keepin' licker in the house, now, heh? Yes? I thought you was church members last time I saw yuh? You always had to send out and get licker then."

"Well, we's expectin' company some of the times these days," smiling teeth like bright-white rays of moon, Betsy, nearly twenty, and still pretty.

"You usin' rouge, too, ain't yuh?"

"Sweet rouge."

"Ya?"

"Yeah, man, sweet and red like your hair."

"Ya?"

No such wise cracking three years ago. Too young and dumb for flirtation then: Betsy. Never like the old woman, talkative, "This here rum come right off de boats from Bermudy. Taste it, Mister Clarence. Strong enough to knock a mule down. Have a glass."

"Here's to you, Mister Clarence."

"Drinkin' licker, too, heh? Hell of a baby, ain't

yuh? Yuh wouldn't even do that last time I saw yuh."

"Sure wouldn't, Mister Clarence, but three years a long time."

"Don't Mister Clarence *me* so much. Yuh know I christened yuh. . . . Auntie, yuh right about this bein' good licker."

"Yes, suh, I knowed you'd like it. It's strong."

"Sit on my lap, kid."

"Sure. . . ."

Soft heavy hips. Hot and browner than the moon —good licker. Drinking it down in little nigger house Florida coast palm fronds scratching roof hum mosquitoes night bugs flies ain't loud enough to keep a man named Clarence girl named Betsy old woman named Auntie from talking and drinking in a little nigger house on Florida coast dead warm night with the licker browner and more fiery than the moon. Yeah, man! A blanket of stars in the Florida sky—outside. In oil-lamp house you don't see no stars. Only a white man with red hair—third mate on a lousy tramp, a nigger girl, and Auntie wrinkled as an alligator bringing the fourth bottle of licker and everybody drinking—when the door . . . slowly . . . opens.

"Say, what the hell? Who's openin' that room door, peepin' in here? It can't be openin' itself?"

The white man stares intently, looking across the table, past the lamp, the licker bottles, the glasses and the old woman, way past the girl. Standing in the door from the kitchen—Look! a damn red-headed baby. Standing not saying a damn word, a damn runt of a red-headed baby.

"What the hell?"

"You Clar—— . . . Mister Clarence, 'cuse me! . . . You hatian, you, get back to you' bed this minute—fo' I tan you in a inch o' yo' life!"

"Ma, let him stay."

Betsy's red-headed child stands in the door looking like one of those goggly-eyed dolls you hit with a ball at the County Fair. The child's face got no change in it. Never changes. Looks like never will change. Just staring—blue-eyed. Hell! God damn! A red-headed blue-eyed yellow-skinned baby!

"You Clarence! . . . 'Cuse me, Mister Clarence. I ain't talkin' to you suh. . . . You, Clarence, go to bed. . . . That chile near 'bout worries de soul-case out o' me. Betsy spiles him, that's why. De po' little thing can't hear, nohow. Just deaf as a post. And over two years old and can't even say, 'Da!' No, suh, can't say, 'Da!' "

"Anyhow, Ma, my child ain't blind."

"Might just as well be blind fo' all de good his eyesight do him. I show him a switch and he don't pay it no mind—'less'n I hit him."

"He's mighty damn white for a nigger child."

"Yes, suh, Mister Clarence. He really ain't got much colored blood in him, a-tall. Betsy's papa,

Mister Clarence, now he were a white man, too. . . . Here, lemme pour you some licker. Drink, Mister Clarence, drink."

Damn little red-headed stupid-faced runt of a child, named Clarence. Bow-legged as hell, too. Three shots for a quarter like a loaded doll in a County Fair. Anybody take a chance. For Christ's sake, stop him from walking across the floor! Will yuh?

"Hey! Take your hands off my legs, you lousy little bastard!"

"He can't hear you, Mister Clarence."

"Tell him to stop crawlin' around then under the table before I knock his block off."

"You varmint. . . ."

"Hey! Take him up from there, will you?"

"Yes, suh, Mister Clarence."

"Hey!"

"You little . . ."

"Hurry! Go on! Get him out then! What's he doin' crawlin' round dumb as hell lookin' at me up at me. I said, *me.* Get him the hell out of here! Hey, Betsy, get him out!"

A red-headed baby. Moonlight-gone baby. No kind of yellow-white bow-legged goggled-eyed County Fair baseball baby. Get him the hell out of here pulling at my legs looking like me at me like me at myself like me red-headed as me.

"Christ!"

"Christ!"

Knocking over glasses by the oil lamp on the table where the night flies flutter Florida where skeleton houses left over from boom sand in the road and no lights in the nigger section across the railroad's knocking over glasses at edge of town where a moon-colored girl's got a red-headed baby deaf as a post like the dolls you wham at three shots for a quarter in the County Fair half full of licker and can't hit nothing.

"Lemme pay for those drinks, will yuh? How much is it?"

"Ain't you gonna stay, Mister Clarence?"

"Lemme pay for my licker, I said."

"Ain't you gonna stay all night?"

"Lemme pay for that licker."

"Why, Mister Clarence? You stayed before."

"How much is the licker?"

"Two dollars, Mister Clarence."

"Here."

"Thank you, Mister Clarence."

"Go'bye!"

"Go'bye."

IX

POOR LITTLE BLACK FELLOW

AMANDA LEE HAD BEEN A PERFECT SERVANT. And her husband Arnold likewise. That the Lord had taken them both so soon was a little beyond understanding. But then, of course, the Lord was just. And He had left the Pembertons poor little black Arnie as their Christian duty. There was no other way to consider the little colored boy whom they were raising as their own, *their very own,* except as a Christian duty. After all, they were white. It was no easy thing to raise a white child, even when it belonged to one, whereas this child was black, and had belonged to their servants, Amanda and Arnold.

But the Pembertons were never known to shirk a duty. They were one of New England's oldest families, one of the finest. They were wealthy. They had a family tree. They had a house in a charming maple-shaded town a few hours from Boston, a cottage at the beach, and four servants. On Tuesdays and Fridays Mr. Pemberton went to town. He had an office of some sort there. But the ladies, Grace Pemberton and her sister, sat on the wide porch at home and crocheted. Or maybe they let James take them for a drive in the car. One of them sang in the choir.

Sometimes they spoke about the two beautiful Negro servants they once had, Amanda and Arnold. They liked to tell poor little Arnie how faithful and lovely his parents had been in life. It would encourage the boy. At present, of course, all their servants were white. Negroes were getting so unsteady. You couldn't keep them in the villages any more. In fact, there were none in Mapleton now. They all went running off to Boston or New York, sporting their money away in the towns. Well, Amanda and Arnold were never like that. They had been simple, true, honest, hard-working. Their qualities had caused the Pembertons to give, over a space of time, more than ten thousand dollars to a school for Negroes at Hampton, Va. Because they thought they saw in Amanda and Arnold the real qualities of an humble and gentle race. That, too, was why they had decided to keep Arnie, poor little black fellow.

The Pembertons had lost nobody in the war except Arnold, their black stable man, but it had been almost like a personal loss. Indeed, after his death, they had kept horses no longer. And the stable had been turned into a garage.

Amanda, his wife, had grieved terribly, too. She had been all wrapped up in Arnold, and in her work with the Pembertons (she was their housekeeper) and in her little dark baby, Arnold, Junior. The child was five when his father went to war; and six when Amanda died of pneumonia a few weeks after they learned Arnold had been killed in the Argonne. The Pembertons were proud of him. A Negro who died for his country. But when that awful Winter of 1919 ended (the Pembertons judged it must have been awful from what they read), when that Winter ended the family was minus two perfect servants who could never come back. And they had on their hands an orphan.

"Poor little black fellow," said Grace Pemberton to her husband and her sister. "In memory of Arnold and Amanda, I think it is our Christian duty to keep it, and raise it up in the way it should go." Somehow, for a long time she called Arnie "it".

"We can raise it, without keeping it," said her husband. "Why not send it to Hampton?"

"Too young for that," said Emily, Mrs. Pemberton's sister. "I have been to Hampton, and they don't take them under twelve there."

So it was decided to keep the little black boy right in Mapleton, to send him to the village school, and to raise him up a good Christian and a good worker. And, it must be admitted, things went pretty well for some years. The white servants were kind to Arnie. The new housekeeper, a big-bosomed Irish woman who came after Amanda's death, treated him as though he were her very own, washed him and fed him. Indeed, they all treated him as if he were their very own.

II

Mr. Pemberton took Arnie to Boston once a season and bought him clothes. On his birthday, they gave him a party—on the lawn—because, after all, his birthday came in the Spring, and there was no need of filling the living-room with children. There was much more room on the lawn. In Summer Arnie went to the sea-shore with the rest of the family.

And Arnie, dark as he was, thrived. He grew up. He did well in his classes. He did well at home, helped with the chores about the house, raked the yard in the Fall, and shoveled snow when the long Winters set in. On Sundays he went to church with the family, listened to a dry and intelligent sermon, chanted the long hymns, and loved the anthems in which Miss Emily sang the solo parts.

Arnie, in church, a little black spot in a forest of white heads above stiff pews. Arnie, out of church, a symbol of how Christian charity should really be administered in the true spirit of the human brotherhood.

The church and the Pembertons were really a little proud of Arnie. Did they not all accept him as their own? And did they not go out of their way to be nice to him—a poor little black fellow whom they, through Christ, had taken in? Throughout the years the whole of Mapleton began to preen itself on its charity and kindness to Arnie. One would think that nobody in the town need ever again do a good deed: that this acceptance of a black boy was quite enough.

Arnie realized how they felt, but he didn't know what to do about it. He kept himself quiet and inconspicuous, and studied hard. He was very grateful, and very lonely. There were no other colored children in the town. But all the grown-up white people made their children be very nice to him, always very nice. "Poor little black boy," they said. "An orphan, and colored. And the Pembertons are so good to him. You be nice to him, too, do you hear? Share your lunch with him. And don't fight him. Or hurt his feelings. He's only a poor little Negro who has no parents." So even the children were over-kind to Arnie.

Everything might have been all right forever had not Arnie begun to grow up. The other children began to grow up, too. Adolescence. The boys had girls. They played kissing games, and learned to dance. There were parties to which Arnie was not invited—really couldn't be invited—with the girls and all. And after generations of peace the village of Mapleton, and the Pembertons, found themselves beset with a Negro problem. Everyone was a little baffled and a little ashamed.

To tell the truth, everybody had got so used to Arnie that nobody really thought of him as a Negro —until he put on long trousers and went to high-school. Now they noticed that he was truly very black. And his voice suddenly became deep and mannish, even before the white boys in Arnie's class talked in the cracks and squeaks of coming manhood.

Then there had arisen that problem of the Boy Scouts. When Arnie was sixteen the Pembertons applied for him to be admitted to a Summer camp for the Scouts at Barrow Beach, and the camp had refused. In a personal letter to Mr. Pemberton, they said they simply could not admit Negroes. Too many parents would object. So several of Arnie's friends and classmates went off to camp in June, and Arnie could not go. The village of Mapleton and the Pembertons felt awfully apologetic for American democracy's attitude to Arnie, whose father had died in the War. But, after all, they couldn't control the Boy Scout Camp. It was a semi-private institution. They were extra nice to Arnie, though—everybody.

That Summer, the Pembertons bought him a bicycle. And toward the end of the Summer (because they thought it was dull for him at the bungalow) they sent him to a Negro charity camp near Boston. It would be nice for him to come to know some of his own people. But Arnie hated it. He stayed a week and came home. The charity camp was full of black kids from the slums of Boston who cussed and fought and made fun of him because he didn't know how to play the dozens. So Arnie, to whom Negroes were a new nation, even if he was black, was amazed and bewildered, and came home. The Pembertons were embarrassed to find him alone in his attic room in the big empty house when they and the servants returned from the beach.

But they wanted so to be nice to him. They asked him if he'd met any friends he'd like to ask down for a week-end. They thought they would give him the whole top floor of the garage that year for a little apartment of his own and he could have his colored friends there. But Arnie hadn't met anyone he wanted to have. He had no colored friends.

The Pembertons knew that he couldn't move in the social world of Mapleton much longer. He was too big. But, really, what could they do? Grace Pemberton prayed. Emily talked it over with the mission board at church, and Mr. Pemberton spoke to the Urban League in Boston. Why not send him to Hampton now?

Arnie had only one more year in the high-school. Then, of course, he would go to college. But to one of the nicer Negro colleges like Fisk, they decided, where those dear Jubilee singers sang so beautifully, and where he would be with his own people, and wouldn't be embarrassed. No, Fisk wasn't as good as Harvard, they knew, but then Arnie had to find his own world after all. They'd have to let him go, poor black fellow! Certainly, he was their very own! But in Mapleton, what could he do, how could he live, whom could he marry? The Pembertons were a bit worried, even, about this one more year. So they decided to be extra nice to him. Indeed, everybody in Mapleton decided to be extra nice to him.

The two rooms over the garage made a fine apartment for a growing boy. His pennants and books and skis were there. Sometimes the white boys came in the evenings and played checkers and smoked forbidden cigarettes. Sometimes they walked out and met the girls at the soda-fountain in Dr. Jourdain's drug-store, and Arnie had a soda with the group. But he always came away alone, while the others went off in pairs. When the Christmas parties were being given, many of the girls were lovely in dresses that looked almost like real evening gowns, but Arnie wasn't invited anywhere but to the Allens'. (And they really didn't count in Mapleton—they were very poor white folks.)

The Pembertons were awfully sorry, of course. They were one of New England's oldest families, and they were raising Arnie as their son. But he was an African, a nice Christian African, and he ought to move among his own people. There he could be a good influence and have a place. The Pembertons couldn't help it that there were no Negroes in Mapleton. Once there had been some, but now they had all moved away. It was more fashionable to have white help. And even as a servant in Mapleton, Arnie would have been a little out of place. But he was smart in school, and a good clean boy. He sang well. (All Negroes were musical.) He skated and swam and played ball. He loved and obeyed the Pembertons. They wanted him to find his place in the world, poor fine little black fellow. Poor dear Arnie.

So it was decided that he would go to Fisk next year. When Arnie agreed, the Pembertons breathed a sort of sigh of joy. They thought he might remember the camp at Boston, and not want to go to a Negro college.

III

And now the Summer presented itself, the last Summer before they let Arnie go away—the boy whom they'd raised as their own. They didn't want that last Summer spoiled for him. Or for them. They wanted no such incidents as the Boy Scout business. The Pembertons were kind people. They wanted Arnie to remember with pleasure his life with them.

Maybe it would be nice to take him to Europe. They themselves had not been abroad for a long

time. Arnie could see Paris and his father's grave
and the Tower of London. The Pembertons would
enjoy the trip, too. And on their return, Arnie
could go directly to Fisk, where his life at college,
and in the grown-up world, would begin. Maybe
he'd marry one of those lovely brown girls who sang
spirituals so beautifully, and live a good Christian
man—occasionally visiting the Pembertons, and
telling them about his influence on the poor black
people of the South.

Graduation came. Arnie took high honors in the
class, and spoke on the program. He went to the
senior prom, but he didn't dance with any of the
girls. He just sort of stood around the punch-bowl,
and joked with the fellows. So nobody was embarrassed, and everyone was glad to see him there. The
one dark spot in a world of whiteness. It was too bad
he didn't have a partner to stand with him when
they sang the Alma Mater after the final dance. But
he was a lucky chap to be going to Europe. Not
many youngsters from Mapleton had been. The
Pembertons were doing well by him, everybody
said aloud, and the church board had got him into
Fisk.

But with all their careful planning, things
weren't going so well about the European trip.
When the steamship company saw the passports,
they cancelled the cabin that had been engaged for
Arnie. Servants always went second class, they

wrote. That Arnie wasn't a servant, it was revealed ultimately, made no difference. He was a Negro, wasn't he?

So it ended with the Pembertons going first, and Arnie second class on the same boat. They would have all gone second, out of sympathy for Arnie, except that accommodations in that class had been completely booked for months ahead. Only as a great favor to first-class passengers had the steamship company managed to find a place for Arnie at all. The Pembertons and their boy had a cross to bear, but they bore it like Christians. At Cherbourg they met the little black fellow again on an equal footing. The evening found them in Paris.

Paris, loveliest of cities, where at dusk the lights are a great necklace among the trees of the Champs Elysées. Paris, song-city of the world. Paris, with the lips of a lovely woman kissing without fear. June, in Paris.

The Pembertons stopped at one of the best hotels. They had a suite which included a room for Arnie. Everything was very nice. The Louvre and the Eiffel Tower and the Café de la Paix were very nice. All with Arnie. Very nice. Everything would have gone on perfectly, surely; and there would have been no story, and Arnie and the Pembertons would have continued in Christian love forever— Arnie at Fisk, of course, and the Pembertons at Mapleton, then Arnie married and the Pembertons growing old, and so on and on—had not Claudina Lawrence moved into the very hotel where the Pembertons were staying. Claudina Lawrence! My God!

True, they had all seen dark faces on the boulevards, and a Negro quartet at the Olympia, but only very good Americans and very high English people were staying at this hotel with the Pembertons. Then Claudina Lawrence moved in—the Claudina who had come from Atlanta, Georgia, to startle the Old World with the new beauty of brown flesh behind footlights. That Claudina who sang divinely and danced like a dryad and had amassed a terrible amount of fame and money in five years. Even the Pembertons had heard of Claudina Lawrence in the quiet and sedate village of Mapleton. Even Arnie had heard of her. And Arnie had been a little bit proud. She was a Negro.

But why did she have to move next door to the Pembertons in this hotel? "Why, Lord, oh, why?" said Grace Pemberton. "For the sake of Arnie, why?" But here the tale begins.

IV

A lot of young Negroes, men and women, shiny and well-dressed, with good and sophisticated manners, came at all hours to see Claudina. Arnie and the Pembertons would meet them in the hall. They were a little too well dressed to suit the Pembertons. They came with white people among them, too— very pretty French girls. And they were terribly lively and gay and didn't seem dependent on anybody. Their music floated out of the windows on the Summer night. The Pembertons hoped they wouldn't get hold of Arnie. They would be a bad influence.

But they did get hold of Arnie.

One morning, as he came out to descend to the lobby to buy post-cards, Claudina herself stepped into the hall at the same time. They met at the elevator. She was the loveliest creature Arnie had ever seen. In pink, all tan and glowing. And she was colored.

"Hello," she said to the young black boy who looked old enough to be less shy. "You look like a home-towner."

"I'm from Mapleton," Arnie stuttered.

"You sound like you're from London," said Claudina, noting his New England accent and confusing it with Mayfair. "But your face says Alabama."

"Oh, I'm colored all right," said Arnie, happy to be recognized by one of his own. "And I'm glad to know you."

"Having a good time?" asked Claudina, as the elevator came.

"No," Arnie said, suddenly truthful. "I don't know anybody."

"Jesus!" said Claudina, sincerely. "That's a shame. A lot of boys and girls are always gathering in my place. Knock on the door some time. I can't see one of my down-home boys getting the blues in Paris. Some of the fellows in my band'll take you around a bit, maybe. They know all the holes and corners. Come in later."

"Thanks awfully," said Arnie.

Claudina left him half-dazed in the lobby. He saw her get into her car at the curb, saw the chauffeur tip his hat, and then drive away. For the first time in his life Arnie was really happy. Somebody had offered him something without charity, without condescension, without prayer, without distance, and without being nice.

All the pictures in the Luxembourg blurred before his eyes that afternoon, and Miss Emily's explanations went in one ear and out the other. He was thinking about Claudina and the friends he might meet in her rooms, the gay and well-dressed Negroes he had seen in the hall, the Paris they could show him, the girls they would be sure to know.

That night he went to see Claudina. He told the Pembertons he didn't care about going to the Odéon, so they went without him, a little reluctantly—because they didn't care about going either, really. They had been sticking rather strenuously to their program of cultural Paris. They were tired. Still, the Pembertons went to the Odéon—it was a play they really should see—and Arnie went next door to Claudina's. But only after he was sure the Pembertons were sitting in the theatre.

Claudina was playing whist. A young Englishman was her partner. Two sleek young colored men were their opponents. "Sit down, honey," Claudina said as if she had known Arnie for years. "You can take a hand in a minute, if you'd like to play. Meet Mr. So and so and so. . . ." She introduced him to the group. "It's kinda early yet. Most of our gang are at work. The theatres aren't out. . . . Marie, bring him a drink." And the French maid poured a cocktail.

A knock, and a rather portly brown-skinned woman, beautifully dressed, entered. "Hello! Who's holding all the trump cards? Glad to meet you, Mr. Arnie. From Boston, you say? My old stamping-ground. Do you know the Roundtrees there?"

"No'm," Arnie said.

"Well, I used to study at the Conservatory and knew all the big shots," the brown-skin woman went on. "Did you just come over? Tourist, heh? Well, what's new in the States now? I haven't been home for three years. Don't intend to go soon. The color-line's a little too much for me. What are they dancing now-a-days? You must've brought a few of the latest steps with you. Can you do the Lindy Hop?"

"No'm," said Arnie.

"Well, I'm gonna see," said the brown-skin lady. She put a record on the victrola, and took Arnie in her arms. Even if he couldn't do the Lindy Hop, he enjoyed dancing with her and they got along famously. Several more people came in, a swell-looking yellow girl, some rather elderly musicians, in spats, and a young colored art student named Harry Jones. Cocktails went around.

"I'm from Chicago," Harry said eventually. "Been over here about a year and like it a hell of a lot. You will, too, soon as you get to know a few folks."

Gradually the room took on the life and gaiety of a party. Somebody sat down at a piano in the alcove, and started a liquid ripple of jazz. Three or four couples began to dance. Arnie and the lovely yellow girl got together. They danced a long time, and then they drank cocktails. Arnie forgot about the clock. It was long after midnight.

Somebody suggested that they all go to the opening of a new Martinique ballroom where a native orchestra would play rattles and drums.

"Come on. Arnie." Harry Jones said. "You

might as well make a night of it. Tomorrow's Sunday."

"I start rehearsals tomorrow," Claudina said, "so I can't go. But listen here," she warned. "Don't you-all take Arnie out of here and lose him. Some of these little French girls are liable to put him in their pockets, crazy as they are about chocolate."

Arnie hoped he wouldn't meet the Pembertons in the hall. He didn't. They were long since in bed. And when Arnie came in at dawn, his head was swimming with the grandest night he'd ever known.

At the Martinique ball he'd met dozens of nice girls: white girls and brown girls, and yellow girls, artists and students and dancers and models and tourists. Harry knew everybody. And everybody was gay and friendly. Paris and music and cocktails made you forget what color people were—and what color you were yourself. Here it didn't matter—color.

Arnie went to sleep dreaming about a little Rumanian girl named Vivi. Harry said she was a music student. But Arnie didn't care what she was, she had such soft black hair and bright grey eyes. How she could dance! And she knew quite a little English. He'd taken her address. Tomorrow he would go to see her. Aw, hell, tomorrow the Pembertons wanted to go to Versailles!

V

When Arnie woke up it was three o'clock. This time Grace Pemberton had actually banged on the door. Arnie was frightened. He'd never slept so late before. What would the Pembertons think?

"What ever is the matter, Arnold?" Mrs. Pemberton called. Only when she was put out did she call him Arnold.

"Up late reading," Arnie muttered through the closed door. "I was up late reading." And then was promptly ashamed of himself for having lied.

"Well, hurry up," Mrs. Pemberton said. "We're about to start for Versailles."

"I don't want to go," said Arnie.

"What ever is the matter with you, boy?" gasped Grace Pemberton.

Arnie had slipped on a bathrobe, so he opened the door.

"Good morning," he said. "I've met some friends. I want to go out with them."

The contrariness of late adolescence was asserting itself. He felt stubborn and mean.

"Friends?" said Grace Pemberton. "What friends, may I ask?"

"A colored student and some others."

"Where did you meet them?"

"Next door, at Miss Lawrence's."

Grace Pemberton stiffened like a bolt. "Get ready, young man," she said, "and come with us to Versailles." She left the room. The young man got ready.

Arnie pouted, but he went with the Pembertons. The sun gave him a headache, and he didn't give a damn about Versailles. That evening, after a private lecture by Mr. Pemberton on the evils of Paris (Grace and Emily had spoken about the beauty of the city), he went to bed feeling very black and sick.

For several days, he wasn't himself at all, what with constant excursions to museums and villages and chateaux, when he wanted to be with Vivi and Harry and Claudina. (Once he did sneak away with Harry to meet Vivi.) Meanwhile, the Pembertons lectured him on his surliness. They were inclined to be dignified and distant to the poor little black fellow now. After all, it had cost them quite a lot to bring him to Paris. Didn't he appreciate what they were doing for him? They had raised him. Had they then no right to forbid him going about with a crowd of Negroes from the theatres?

"He's a black devil," said Mr. Pemberton.

"Poor little fellow," said Grace. She was a little sorry for him.

"After all, he doesn't know. He's young. Let us just try loving him, and being very nice to him."

So once again the Pembertons turned loose on

Arnie their niceness. They took him to the races, and they bought him half a dozen French ties from a good shop, and they treated him better than if he were their own.

But Arnie was worse than ever. He stayed out all night one night. Grace knew, because she knocked on his door at two o'clock. And the Negroes next door, how they laughed! How they danced! How the music drifted through the windows. It seemed as if the actual Devil had got into Arnie. Was he going to the dogs before their very eyes? Grace Pemberton was worried. After all, he *was* the nearest thing she'd ever had to a son. She was really fond of him.

As for Arnie, it wasn't the Devil at all that had got him. It wasn't even Claudina. It was Vivi, the little girl he'd met through Harry at the Martinique ball. The girl who played Chopin on the piano, and had grey eyes and black hair and came from Rumania. By himself, Arnie had managed to find, from the address she had given him, the tall house near the Parc Monceau where she lived in an attic room. Up six flights of stairs he walked. He found her with big books on theory in front of her and blank music pages, working out some sort of exercise in harmony. Her little face was very white, her grey eyes very big, and her black hair all fluffy around her head. Arnie didn't know why he had come to see her except that he liked her very much.

They talked all afternoon and Arnie told her about his life at home, how white people had raised him, and how hard it was to be black in America. Vivi said it didn't make any difference in Rumania, or in Paris either, about being black.

"Here it's only hard to be poor," Vivi said.

But Arnie thought he wouldn't mind being poor in a land where it didn't matter what color you were.

"Yes, you would mind," Vivi said.

"Being poor's not easy anywhere. But then," and her eyes grew bigger, "by and by the Revolution will come. In Rumania the Revolution will come. In France, too. Everywhere poor people are tired of being poor."

"What Revolution?" Arnie asked, for he hadn't heard about it in Mapleton.

Vivi told him.

"Where we live, it's quiet," he said. "My folks come from Massachusetts."

VI

And then the devil whispered to Arnie. Maybe Vivi would like to meet some real Americans. Anyway, he would like the Pembertons to meet her. He'd like to show them that there actually was a young white girl in the world who didn't care about color. They were always educating him. He would educate them a bit. So Arnie invited Vivi to dinner at the hotel that very night.

The Pembertons had finished their soup when he entered the sparkling dining-room of the hotel. He made straight for their table. The orchestra was playing Strauss. Gentlemen in evening clothes and ladies in diamonds scanned a long and expensive menu. The Pembertons looked up and saw Arnie coming, guiding Vivi by the hand. Grace Pemberton gasped and put her spoon back in the soup. Emily went pale. Mr. Pemberton's mouth opened. All the Americans stared. Such a white, white girl and such a black, black boy coming across the dining-room floor! The girl had a red mouth and grey eyes.

The Pembertons had been waiting for Arnie since four o'clock. Today a charming Indian mystic, Nadjuti, had come to tea with them, especially to see the young Negro student they had raised in America. The Pembertons were not pleased that Arnie had not been there.

"This is my friend," Arnie said. "I've brought her to dinner."

Vivi smiled and held out her hand, but the Pembertons bowed in their stiffest fashion. Nobody noticed her hand.

"I'm sorry," said Grace Pemberton, "but there's room for only four at our table."

"Oh," said Arnie. He hadn't thought they'd be

rude. Polite and formal, maybe, but not rude. "Oh! Don't mind us then. Come on, Vivi." His eyes were red as he led her away to a vacant table by the fountain. A waiter came and took their orders with the same deference he showed everyone else. The Pembertons looked and could not eat.

"Where ever did he get her?" whispered Emily in her thin New England voice, as her cheeks burned. "Is she a woman from the streets?" The Pembertons couldn't imagine that so lovely a white girl would go out with a strange Negro unless she were a prostitute. They were terribly mortified. What would he do next?

"But maybe he doesn't know. Did you warn him, John?" Grace Pemberton addressed her husband.

"I did," replied Mr. Pemberton shortly.

"A scarlet woman," said Emily faintly. "A scarlet . . . I think I shall go to my room. All the Americans in the dining-room must have seen." She was white as she rose. "We've been talked about enough as it is—travelling with a colored boy. For our sakes, he might have been careful."

The Pembertons left the dining-room. But Grace Pemberton was afraid for Arnie. Near the door, she turned and came over to the table by the fountain. "Please, Arnold, come to my room before you go."

"Yes, Miss Grace, I'll come," he said.

"You mustn't mind." Vivi patted his arm. The

orchestra was playing "The Song of India." "All old people are the same."

As they ate, Vivi and Arnie talked about parents. Vivi told him how her folks hadn't allowed her to come away to study music, how they'd even tried to stop her at the station. "Most elderly people are terrible," she said, "especially parents."

"But they're not my parents," Arnie said. "They are white people."

When he took Vivi home, he kissed her. Then he came back and knocked on the living-room door.

VII

"Come in," Grace Pemberton said. "Come in, Arnie, I want to talk to you." She was sitting there alone, very straight with her iron-grey hair low on her neck. "Poor little black fellow," she said, as through Arnie had done a great and careless wrong. "Come here."

When Arnie saw her pale white face from the door, he was a little sad and ashamed that he might have done something to hurt her. But when she began to pity him, "poor little black fellow", a sudden anger shook him from head to foot. His eyes grew sultry and red, his spirit stubborn.

"Arnold," she said, "I think we'd better go home, back to America."

"I don't want to go," he replied.

"But you don't seem to appreciate what we are doing for you here," she said, "at all."

"I don't," Arnie answered.

"You don't!" Grace Pemberton's throat went dry. "You don't? We're showing you the best of Paris, and you don't? Why, we've done all we could for you always, Arnie boy. We've raised you as our own. And we want to do more. We're going to send you to college, of course, to Fisk this Fall."

"I don't want to go to Fisk," Arnie said.

"What?"

"No," said Arnie. "I don't want to go. It'll be like that camp in Boston. Everything in America's like that camp in Boston." His eyes grew redder. "Separate, segregated, shut-off! Black people kept away from everybody else. I go to Fisk; my classmates, Harvard and Amherst and Yale . . . I sleep in the garage, you sleep in the house."

"Oh," Grace Pemberton said. "We didn't mean it like that!"

Arnie was being cruel, just cruel. She began, in spite of herself, to cry.

"I don't want to go back home," Arnie went on. "I hate America."

"But your father *died* for America," Grace Pemberton cried.

"I guess he was a fool," said Arnie.

The hall door opened. Mr. Pemberton and his sister-in-law came in from a walk through the park.

They saw Mrs. Pemberton's eyes wet, and Arnie's sultry face. Mrs. Pemberton told them what he'd said.

"So you want to stay here," said Mr. Pemberton, trying to hold his temper. "Well, stay. Take your things and stay. Stay now. Get out! Go!

Anger possessed him, fury against this ungrateful black boy who made his wife cry. Grace Pemberton never cried over anything Mr. Pemberton did. And now, she was crying over this . . . this . . . In the back of his mind was the word *nigger*. Arnold felt it.

"I want to go," said Arnie. "I've always wanted to go."

"You little black fool!" said Emily.

"Where will you go?" Grace Pemberton asked. Why, oh why, didn't Arnie say he was sorry, beg their pardon, and stay? He knew he could if he wanted to.

"I'll go to Vivi," Arnie said.

"Vivi?" a weak voice gasped.

"Yes, marry Vivi!"

"Marry white, eh?" said Mr. Pemberton. Emily laughed drily. But Grace Pemberton fainted.

Next door, just then, the piano was louder than ever. Somebody was doing a tap dance. The dancing and the music floated through the windows on the soft Paris air. Outside, the lights were a necklace

of gold over the Champs Elysées. Autos honked.
Trees rustled. People passed.

Arnie went out.

LITTLE DOG

Miss Briggs had a little apartment all alone in a four story block just where Oakwood Drive curved past the park and the lake. Across the street, beneath her window, kids skated in winter, and in the spring the grass grew green. In summer, lovers walked and necked by the lake in the moonlight. In fall brown and red-gold leaves went skithering into the water when the wind blew.

Miss Briggs came home from work every night at eight, unless she went to the movies or the Women's Civics Club. On Sunday evenings she sometimes went to a lecture on Theosophy. But she was never one to gad about, Miss Briggs. Besides she worked too hard. She was the head bookkeeper for the firm of Wilkins and Bryant, Wood, Coal And Coke. And since 1930, when they had cut down the staff, she had only one assistant. Just two of them now to take care of the books, bills, and everything. But Miss Briggs was very efficient. She had been head bookkeeper for twenty-one years. Wilkins and Bryant didn't know what they would do without her.

Miss Briggs was proud of her record as a book-keeper. Once the City Hall had tried to get her, but Wilkins and Bryant said, "No, indeed. We can pay as much as the city, if not more. You stay right here with us." Miss Briggs stayed. She was never a person to move about much or change jobs.

As a young girl she had studied very hard in business school. She never had much time to go out. A widowed mother, more or less dependent on her then, later became completely dependent—paralyzed. Her mother had been dead for six years now.

Perhaps it was the old woman's long illness that had got Miss Briggs in the habit of staying home every night in her youth, instead of going out to the theatre or to parties. They had never been able to afford a maid even after Miss Briggs became so well paid—for doctors' bills were such a drain, and in those last months a trained nurse was needed for her mother—God rest her soul.

Now, alone, Miss Briggs usually ate her dinner in the Rose Bud Tea Shoppe. A number of genteel business women ate there, and the colored waiters were so nice. She had been served by Joe or Perry, flat-footed old Negro gentlemen, for three or four years now. They knew her tastes, and would get the cook to make little special dishes for her if she wasn't feeling very well.

After dinner, with a walk of five or six blocks

from the Rose Bud, the park would come into view
with its trees and lights. The Lyle Apartments
loomed up. A pretty place to live, facing the park.
Miss Briggs had moved there after her mother died.
Trying to keep house alone was just a little too
much. And there was no man in view to marry.
Most of them would want her only for her money
now, at her age, anyway. To move with another
woman, Miss Briggs thought, would be a sort of
sacrilege so soon after her mother's death. Besides,
she really didn't know any other woman who, like
herself, was without connections. Almost everybody
had somebody, Miss Briggs reflected. Every woman
she knew had either a husband, or sisters, or a friend
of long standing with whom she resided. But Miss
Briggs had nobody at all. Nobody.

Not that she thought about it very much. Miss
Briggs was too used to facing the world alone, minding her own business, and going her own way. But
one summer, while returning from Michigan
where she had taken her two weeks' rest, as she
came through Cleveland, on her way from the boat
to the station there, she happened to pass a dog
shop with a window full of fuzzy little white dogs.
Miss Briggs called to the taxi man to stop. She got
out and went in. When she came back to the taxi,
she carried a little white dog named Flips. At least,
the dealer said he had been calling it Flips because
its ears were so floppy.

"They just flip and flop," the man said, smiling at the tall middle-aged woman.

"How much is he?" Miss Briggs asked, holding the puppy up.

"I'll let you have him for twenty-five dollars," the man said.

Miss Briggs put the puppy down. She thought that was a pretty steep price. But there was something about Flips that she liked, so she picked him up again and took him with her. After all, she allowed herself very few indulgences. And somehow, this summer, Miss Briggs sort of hated going back to an empty flat—even if it did overlook the park.

Or maybe it was because it overlooked the park that had made it so terrible a place to live lately. Miss Briggs had never felt lonely, not *very* lonely, in the old house after her mother died. Only when she moved to the flat, did her loneliness really come down on her. There were some nights there, especially summer nights, when she thought she couldn't stand it, to sit in her window and see so many people going by, couple by couple, arms locked; or else in groups, laughing and talking. Miss Briggs wondered why she knew no one, male or female, to walk out with, laughing and talking. She knew only the employees where she worked, and with whom she associated but little (for she hated to have people know her business). She knew, of course, the members of the Women's Civics Club, but in a cultural sort of way. The warmth of friendship seldom mellowed her contacts there. Only one or two of the club women had ever called on her. Miss Briggs always believed in keeping her distance, too. Her mother used to say she'd been born poor but proud, and would stay that way.

"Folks have to amount to something before Clara takes up with them," old Mrs. Briggs always said. "Men'll have a hard time getting Clara."

Men did. Now, with no especial attractions to make them keep trying, Miss Briggs, tall and rail-like, found herself left husbandless at an age when youth had gone.

So, in her forty-fifth year, coming back from a summer boarding house in Michigan, Miss Briggs bought herself a little white dog. When she got home, she called on the janitor and asked him to bring her up a small box for Flips. The janitor, a tow-headed young Swede, brought her a grapefruit crate from the A. & P. Miss Briggs put it in the kitchen for Flips.

She told the janitor to bring her, too, three times a week, a dime's worth of dog meat or bones, and leave it on the back porch where she could find it when she came home. On other nights, Flips ate dog biscuits.

Flips and Miss Briggs soon settled on a routine.

Each evening when she got home she would feed him. Then she would take him for a walk. This gave Miss Briggs an excuse for getting out, too. In warm weather she would walk around the little lake fronting her apartment with Flips on a string. Sometimes she would even smile at other people walking around the lake with dogs at night. It was nice the way dogs made things friendly. It was nice the way people with dogs smiled at her occasionally because she had a dog, too. But whenever (as seldom happened) someone in the park, dog or no dog, tried to draw her into conversation, Miss Briggs would move on as quickly as she could without being rude. You could never tell just who people were, Miss Briggs thought, or what they might have in their minds. No, you shouldn't think of taking up with strange people in parks. Besides, she was head bookkeeper for Wilkins and Bryant, and in these days of robberies and kidnappings maybe they just wanted to find out when she went for the pay roll, and how much cash the firm kept on hand. Miss Briggs didn't trust people.

Always, by ten o'clock, she was back with Flips in her flat. A cup of hot milk then maybe, with a little in a saucer for Flips, and to bed. In the morning she would let Flips run down the back steps for a few minutes, then she gave him more milk, left a pan of water, and went to work. A regular routine, for Miss Briggs took care of Flips with great seriousness. At night when she got back from the Rose Bud Tea Shoppe, she fed him biscuits; or if it were dog meat night, she looked out on the back porch for the package the janitor was paid to leave. (That is, Miss Briggs allowed the Swede fifty cents a week to buy bones. He could keep the change.)

But one night, the meat was not there. Miss Briggs thought perhaps he had forgotten. Still he had been bringing it regularly for nearly two years. Maybe the warm spring this year made the young janitor listless, Miss Briggs mused. She fed Flips biscuits.

But two days later, another dog meat night, the package was not there either. "This is too much!" thought Miss Briggs. "Come on, Flipsy, let's go downstairs and see. I'm sure I gave him fifty cents this week to buy your bones."

Miss Briggs and the little white beast went downstairs to ask why there was no meat for her dog to eat. When they got to the janitor's quarters in the basement, they heard a mighty lot of happy laughter and kids squalling, and people moving. They didn't sound like Swedes, either. Miss Briggs was a bit timid about knocking, but she finally mustered up courage with Flips there beside her. A sudden silence fell inside.

"You Leroy," a voice said. "Go to de door."

A child's feet came running. The door opened

like a flash and a small colored boy stood there grinning.

"Where—where is the janitor?" Miss Briggs said, taken aback.

"You mean my papa?" asked the child, looking at the gaunt white lady. "He's here." And off he went to call his father.

Surrounded by children, a tall broad-shouldered Negro of perhaps forty, gentle of face and a little stooped, came to the door.

"Good evenin'," he said pleasantly.

"Why, are you the janitor?" stammered Miss Briggs. Flips had already begun to jump up on him with friendly mien.

"Yes'm, I'm the new janitor," said the Negro in a softly beautiful voice, kids all around him. "Is there something I can help you to do?"

"Well," said Miss Briggs, "I'd like some bones for my little dog. He's missed his meat two times now. Can you get him some?"

"Yes'm, sure can," said the new janitor, "if all the stores ain't closed." He was so much taller than Miss Briggs that she had to look up at him.

"I'd appreciate it," said Miss Briggs, "please."

As she went back upstairs she heard the new janitor calling in his rich voice, "Lora, you reckon that meat store's still open?" And a woman's voice and a lot of children answered him.

It turned out that the store was closed. So Miss

Briggs gave the Negro janitor ten cents and told him to have the meat there the next night when she came home.

"Flips, you shan't starve," she said to the little white dog, "new janitor or no new janitor."

"Wruff!" said Flips.

But the next day when she came home there was no meat on the back porch either. Miss Briggs was puzzled, and a little hurt. Had the Negro forgotten?

Scarcely had she left the kitchen, however, when someone knocked on the back door and there stood the colored man with the meat. He was almost as old as Miss Briggs, she was certain of it, looking at him. Not a young man at all, but he was awfully big and brown and kind looking. So sort of sure about life as he handed her the package.

"I thought some other dog might get it if I left it on the porch," said the colored man. "So I kept it downstairs till you come."

Miss Briggs was touched. "Well, thank you very much," she said.

When the man had gone, she remembered that she had not told him how often to get meat for the dog.

The next night he came again with bones, and every night from then on. Miss Briggs did not stop him, or limit him to three nights a week. Just after eight, whenever she got home, up the back porch steps the Negro would come with the dog meat.

Sometimes there would be two or three kids with him. Pretty little brown-black rather dirty kids, Miss Briggs thought, who were shy in front of her, but nice.

Once or twice during the spring, the janitor's wife, instead, brought the dog meat up on Saturday nights. Flips barked rudely at her. Miss Briggs didn't take to the creature, either. She was fat and yellow, and certainly too old to just keep on having children as she evidently did. The janitor himself was so solid and big and strong! Miss Briggs felt better when he brought her the bones for her dog. She didn't like his wife.

That June, on warm nights, as soon as she got home, Miss Briggs would open the back door and let the draft blow through. She could hear the janitor better coming up the rear stairs when he brought the bones. And, of course, she never said more than good-evening to him and thank you. Or here's a dollar for the week. Keep the change.

Flips ate an awful lot of meat that spring. "Your little dog's a regular meat-hound," the janitor said one night as he handed her the bones; and Miss Briggs blushed, for no good reason.

"He does eat a lot," she said. "Goodnight."

As she spread the bones out on paper for the dog, she felt that her hands were trembling. She left Flips eating and went into the parlor, but found that she could not keep her mind on the book she was reading. She kept looking at the big kind face of the janitor in her mind, perturbed that it was a Negro face, and that it stayed with her so.

The next night, she found herself waiting for the dog meat to arrive with more anxiety than Flips himself. When the colored man handed it to her, she quickly closed the door, before her face got red again.

"Funny old white lady," thought the janitor as he went back downstairs to his basement full of kids. "Just crazy about that dog," he added to his wife. "I ought to tell her it ain't good to feed a dog so much meat."

"What do you care, long as she wants to?" asked his wife.

The next day in the office Miss Briggs found herself making errors over the books. That night she hurried home to be sure and be there on time when he brought the dog meat up, in case he came early.

"What's the matter with me," she said sharply to herself, "rushing this way just to feed Flips? Whatever is the matter with me?" But all the way through the warm dusky streets, she seemed to hear the janitor's deep voice saying, "Good evenin'," to her.

Then, when the Negro really knocked on the door with the meat, she was trembling so that she could not go to the kitchen to get it. "Leave it right there by the sink," she managed to call out. "Thank you, Joe."

She heard the man going back downstairs sort of humming to himself, a kid or so following him. Miss Briggs felt as if she were going to faint, but Flips kept jumping up on her, barking for his meat.

"Oh, Flips," she said, "I'm so hungry." She meant to say, "*You're* so hungry." So she repeated it. "You're so hungry! Heh, Flipsy, dog?"

And from the way the little dog barked, he must have been hungry. He loved meat.

The next evening, Miss Briggs was standing in the kitchen when the colored man came with the bones.

"Lay them down," she said, "thank you," trying not to look at him. But as he went downstairs, she watched through the window his beautifully heavy body finding the rhythm of the steps, his big brown neck moving just a little.

"Get down!" she said sharply to Flips barking for his dinner.

To herself she said earnestly, "I've got to move. I can't be worried being so far from a meat shop, or from where I eat my dinner. I think I'll move downtown where the shops are open at night. I can't stand this. Most of my friends live downtown anyway."

But even as she said it, she wondered what friends she meant. She had a little white dog named Flips, that was all. And she was acquainted with other people who worked at Wilkins and Bryant, but she had nothing to do with them. She was the head bookkeeper. She knew a few women in the Civics Club fairly well. And the Negro waiters at the Rose Bud Shoppe.

And this janitor!

Miss Briggs decided that she could not bear to have this janitor come upstairs with a package of bones for Flips again. She was sure he was happy down there with his portly yellow wife and his house full of children. Let him stay in the basement, then, where he belonged. She never wanted to see him again, never.

The next night, Miss Briggs made herself go to a movie before coming home. And when she got home, she fed Flips dog biscuits. That week she began looking for a new apartment, a small one for two, her and the dog. Fortunately there were plenty to be had, what with people turned out for not being able to pay their rent—which would never happen to her, thank God! She had saved her money. When she found an apartment, she deposited the first month's rent at once. On her coming Saturday afternoon off, she planned to move.

Friday night, when the janitor came up with the bones, she decided to be just a little pleasant to him. Probably she would never see him again. Perhaps she would give him a dollar for a tip, then. Something to remember her by.

When he came upstairs, she was aware a long

time of his feet approaching. Coming up, up, up, bringing bones for her dog. Flips began to bark. Miss Briggs went to the door. She took the package in one hand. With the other she offered the bill.

"Thank you so much for buying bones for my little dog," she said. "Here, here is a dollar for your trouble. You keep it all."

"Much obliged, m'am," said the astonished janitor. He had never seen Miss Briggs so generous before. "Thank you, m'am! He sure do eat a heap o' bones, your little dog."

"He almost keeps me broke buying bones," Miss Briggs said, holding the door.

"True," said the janitor. "But I reckon you don't have much other expenses on hand, do you? No family and all like me?"

"You're right," answered Miss Briggs. "But a little dog is so much company, too."

"Guess they are, m'am," said the janitor, turning to go. "Well, goodnight, Miss Briggs. I'm much obliged."

"Goodnight, Joe."

As his broad shoulders and tall brown body disappeared down the stairs, Miss Briggs slowly turned her back, shut the door, and put the bones on the floor for Flipsy. Then suddenly she began to cry.

The next day she moved away as she had planned to do. The janitor never saw her any more. For a few days, the walkers in the park beside the lake wondered where a rather gaunt middle-aged woman who used to come out at night with a little white dog had gone. But in a very short while the neighborhood had completely forgotten her.

XI

BERRY

WHEN THE BOY ARRIVED on the four o'clock train, lo and behold, he turned out to be colored! Mrs. Osborn saw him the minute he got out of the station wagon, but certainly there was nothing to be done about it that night—with no trains back to the city before morning—so she set him to washing dishes. Lord knows there were a plenty. The Scandinavian kitchen boy had left right after breakfast, giving no notice, leaving her and the cook to do everything. Her wire to the employment office in Jersey City brought results—but dark ones. The card said his name was Milberry Jones.

Well, where was he to sleep? Heretofore, the kitchen boy and the handy-man gardener-chauffeur shared the same quarters. But Mrs. Osborn had no idea how the handy-man might like Negroes. Help were so touchy, and it was hard keeping good servants in the country. So right after dinner, leaving Milberry with his arms in the dish water, Mrs. Osborn made a bee line across the side lawn for Dr. Renfield's cottage.

She heard the kids laughing and playing on the

big screened-in front porch of the sanatorium. She heard one of the nurses say to a child, "Behave, Billy!" as she went across the yard under the pine and maple trees. Mrs. Osborn hoped Dr. Renfield would be on his porch. She hated to knock at the door and perhaps be faced with his wife. The gossip among the nurses and help at Dr. Renfield's Summer Home for Crippled Children had it that Mrs. Osborn was in love with Dr. Renfield, that she just worshipped him, that she followed him with her eyes every chance she got—and not only with her eyes.

Of course, there wasn't a word of truth in it, Mrs. Osborn said to herself, admitting at the same time that that Martha Renfield, his wife, was certainly not good enough for the doctor. Anyway tonight, she was not bound on any frivolous errand toward the Doctor's cottage. She had to see him about this Negro in their midst. At least, they'd have to keep him there overnight, or until they got somebody else to help in the kitchen. However, he looked like a decent boy.

Dr. Renfield was not at home. His wife came to the door, spoke most coldly, and said that she presumed, as usual, the Doctor would make his rounds of the Home at eight. She hoped Mrs. Osborn could wait until then to see him.

"Good evening!"

Mrs. Osborn went back across the dusk-dark

yard. She heard the surf rushing at the beach below, and saw the new young moon rising. She thought maybe the Doctor was walking along the sea in the twilight alone. Ah, Dr. Renfield, Dr. Ren. . . .

When he made the usual rounds at eight he came, for a moment, by Mrs. Osborn's little office where the housekeeper held forth over her linens and her accounts. He turned his young but bearded face toward Mrs. Osborn, cast his great dark eyes upon her, and said, "I hear you've asked to see me?"

"Yes, indeed, Dr. Renfield," Mrs. Osborn bubbled and gurgled. "We have a problem on our hands. You know the kitchen man left this morning so I sent a wire to the High Class Help Agency in the city for somebody right away by the four o'clock train—and they sent us a Negro! He seems to be a nice boy, and all that, but I just don't know how he would fit in our Home. Now what do you think?"

The doctor looked at her with great seriousness. He thought. Then he answered with a question, "Do the other servants mind?"

"Well, I can't say they do. They got along all right tonight during dinner. But the problem is, where would he sleep?"

"Oh, yes," said Dr. Renfield, pursing his lips.

"And whether we should plan to keep him all summer, or just till we get someone else?"

"I see," said Dr. Renfield.

And again he thought. "You say he can do the work? . . . How about the attic in this building? It's not in use. . . . And by the way, how much did we pay the other fellow?"

"Ten dollars a week," said Mrs. Osborn raising her eyes.

"Well, pay the darkie eight," said Dr. Renfield, "and keep him." And for a moment he gazed deep into Mrs. Osborn's eyes. "Goodnight." Then turned and left her. Left her. Left her.

So it was that Milberry entered into service at Dr. Renfield's Summer Home for Crippled Children.

Milberry was a nice black boy, big, good natured and strong—like what Paul Robeson must have been at twenty. Except that he wasn't educated. He was from Georgia, where they don't have many schools for Negroes. And he hadn't been North long. He was glad to have a job, even if it was at a home for Crippled Children way out in the country on a beach five miles from the nearest railroad. Milberry had been hungry for weeks in Newark and Jersey City. He needed work and food.

And even if he wasn't educated, he had plenty of mother wit and lots of intuition about people and places. It didn't take him long to realize that he was doing far too much work for the Home's eight dollars a week, and that everybody was imposing on him in that taken-for-granted way white folks do with Negro help.

Milberry got up at 5:30 in the mornings, made the fire for the cook, set the water to boiling for the head nurse's coffee, started peeling potatoes, onions, and apples. After breakfast he washed up all the dishes, scoured the pots and pans, scrubbed the floors, and carried in wood for the fireplace in the front room (which really wasn't his job at all, but the handy-man's who had put it off on Milberry). The waitresses, too, got in the habit of asking him to polish their silver, and ice their water. And Mrs. Osborn always had something extra that needed to be done (not kitchen-boy work), a cellar to be cleaned out, or the linen in her closet re-shelved, or the dining-room windows washed. Milberry knew they took him for a work horse, a fool—and a nigger. Still he did everything, and didn't look mad—jobs were too hard to get, and he had been hungry too long in town.

"Besides," Milberry said to himself, "the ways of white folks, I mean some white folks, is too much for me. I reckon they must be a few good ones, but most of 'em ain't good—leastwise they don't treat me good. And Lawd knows, I ain't never done nothin' to 'em, nothin' a-tall."

But at the Home it wasn't the work that really troubled him, or the fact that nobody ever said anything about a day off or a little extra pay. No.

he'd had many jobs like this one before, where they worked you to death. But what really worried Milberry at this place was that he seemed to sense something wrong—something phoney about the whole house—except the little crippled kids there like himself because they couldn't help it. Maybe it was the lonesomeness of that part of the Jersey coast with its pines and scrubs and sand. But, more nearly, Milberry thought it was that there doctor with the movie beard and the woman's eyes at the head of the home. And it was the cranky nurses always complaining about food and the little brats under them. And the constant talk of who was having an affair with Dr. Renfield. And Mrs. Osborn's grand manner to everybody but the doctor. And all the white help kicking about their pay, and how far it was from town, and how no-good the doctor was, or the head nurse, or the cook, or Mrs. Osborn.

"It's sho a phoney, this here place," Milberry said to himself. "Funny how the food ain't nearly so good 'cept when some ma or pa of some chile is visitin' here—then when they gone, it drops right back down again. This here hang-out is jest Doc Renfield's own private gyp game. Po' little children."

The Negro was right. The Summer Home was run for profits from the care of permanently deformed children of middle class parents who couldn't afford to pay too much, but who still paid well—too well for what their children got in return. Milberry worked in the kitchen and saw the good cans opened for company, and the cheap cans opened for the kids. Somehow he didn't like such dishonesty. Somehow, he thought he wouldn't even stay there and work if it wasn't for the kids.

For the children grew terribly to like Milberry.

One afternoon, during his short period of rest between meals, he had walked down to the beach where those youngsters who could drag themselves about were playing, and others were sitting in their wheel chairs watching. The sky was only a little cloudy, and the sand was grey. But quite all of a sudden it began to rain. The nurses saw Milberry and called him to help them get the young ones quickly back to the house. Some of the children were too heavy for a nurse to lift easily into a wheel chair. Some couldn't run at all. The handy-man helper wasn't around. So Milberry picked up child after child, sometimes two at once, and carried them up to the broad screened-in porch of the Home like a big gentle horse. The children loved it, riding on his broad back, or riding in his arms in the soft gentle rain.

"Come and play with us sometimes," one of them called as Milberry left them all on the safe dry porch with their nurses.

"Sure, come back and play," another said.

So Milberry, the next day, went down to the

beach again in the afternoon and played with the crippled children. At first the nurses, Miss Baxter and Mrs. Hill, didn't know whether to let him stay or not, but their charges seemed to enjoy it. Then when the time came to go in for rest before dinner, Milberry helped push the wheel chairs, a task which the nurses hated. And he held the hands of those kids with braces and twisted limbs as they hobbled along. He told them stories, and he made up jokes in the sun on the beach. And one rainy afternoon on the porch he sang songs, old southern Negro songs, funny ones that the children loved.

Almost every afternoon then, Milberry came to the beach after the luncheon dishes were done, and he had washed himself—except those afternoons when Mrs. Osborn found something else for him to do—vases to be emptied or bath tubs scoured. The children became Milberry's friends. They adored him and he them. They called him Berry. They put their arms about him.

The grown-up white folks only spoke to him when they had some job for him to do, or when they were kidding him about being dark, and talking flat and Southern, and mispronouncing words. But the kids didn't care how he talked. They loved his songs and his stories.

And he made up stories out of his own head just for them—po' little crippled-up things that they were—for Berry loved them, too.

So the summer wore on. August came. In September the Home would close. But disaster overtook Milberry before then.

At the end of August a week of rain fell, and the children could not leave the porch. Then, one afternoon, the sun suddenly came out bright and warm. The sea water was blue again and the sand on the beach glistened. Miss Baxter (who by now had got the idea it was part of Milberry's job to help her with the children) went to the kitchen and called him while he was still washing luncheon dishes.

"Berry, we're going to take the children down to the beach. Come on and help us with the chairs as soon as you get through."

"Yes, m'am," said Berry.

When he came out on the porch, the kids were all excited about playing in the sun once more. Little hunchbacks jumped and cried and clapped their hands, and little paralytics laughed in their wheel chairs. And some with braces on had already hobbled out the screen door and were gathered on the walk.

"Hello, Berry," the children called.

"Hey, Berry," they cried to the black boy.

Berry grinned.

It was a few hundred yards to the beach. On the cement walk, you could push a couple of wheel chairs at a time to the sand's edge. Some of the chil-

dren propelled their own. Besides the nurses, today the handy-man was helping for the sun might
not last long.

"Take me," a little boy called from his wheel
chair, "Berry, take me."

"Sho, I will," the young Negro said gently.

But when Berry started to push the chair down
from the porch to the walk, the child, through excess of joy, suddenly leaned forward laughing, and
suddenly lost his balance. Berry saw that he was
going to fall. To try to catch the boy, the young
Negro let the chair go. But quick as a wink, the
child had fallen one way onto the lawn, the chair
the other onto the cement walk. The back of
the chair was broken, snapped off, except for the
wicker. The little boy lay squalling on the ground
in the grass.

Lord have mercy!

All the nurses came running, the handy-man,
and Mrs. Osborn, too. Berry picked up the boy,
who clung to his neck sobbing, more frightened, it
seemed, than hurt.

"Po' little chile," Berry kept saying. "Is you
hurt much? I's so sorry."

But the nurses were very angry, for they were
responsible. And Mrs. Osborn—well, she lit out for
Dr. Renfield.

The little boy still clung to Berry, and wouldn't
let the nurses take him at all. He had stopped cry-

ing when Dr. Renfield arrived, but was still sniffling. He had his arms tight around the black boy's neck.

"Give that child to me," Dr. Renfield said, his brown beard pointing straight at Berry, his mind visualizing irate parents and a big damage suit, and bad publicity for the Home.

But when the doctor tried to take the child, the little boy wriggled and cried and wouldn't let go of Berry. With what strength he had in his crooked braced limbs, he kicked at the doctor.

"Give me that child!" Dr. Renfield shouted at Berry. "Bring him into my office and lay him down." He put on his nose glasses. "You careless black rascal! And you, Miss Baxter—" the doctor shriveled her with a look. "I want to see you."

In the clinic, it turned out that the child wasn't really hurt, though. His legs had been, from birth, twisted and deformed. Nothing could injure them much further. And fortunately his spine wasn't weak.

But the doctor kept saying, "Criminal carelessness! Criminal carelessness!" Mrs. Osborn kept agreeing with him, "Yes, it is! Indeed, it is!" Milberry was to blame.

The black boy felt terrible. But nobody else among the grown-ups seemed to care how he felt. They all said: What dumbness! he had let that child fall!

"Get rid of him," Dr. Renfield said to the house-keeper, "today. The fool nigger! And deduct ten dollars for that broken chair."

"We don't pay him but eight," Mrs. Osborn said.

"Well, deduct that," said the doctor.

So, without his last week's wages, Milberry went to Jersey City.

XII

MOTHER AND CHILD

"AIN'T NOBODY SEEN IT," said old lady Lucy Doves. "Ain't nobody seen it, but the midwife and the doctor, and her husband, I reckon. They say she won't let a soul come in the room. But it's still living, 'cause Mollie Ransom heard it crying. And the woman from Downsville what attended the delivery says it's as healthy a child as she ever seed, indeed she did."

"Well, it's a shame," said Sister Wiggins, "it's here. I been living in Boyd's Center for twenty-two years, at peace with these white folks, ain't had no trouble yet, till this child was born—now look at 'em. Just look what's goin' on! People acting like a pack o' wolves."

"Poor little brat! He ain't been in the world a week yet," said Mrs. Sam Jones, taking off her hat, "and done caused more trouble than all the rest of us in a life time. I was born here, and I ain't never seen the white folks up in arms like they are today. But they don't need to think they can walk over Sam and me—for we owns our land, it's bought and paid for, and we sends our children to school.

Thank God, this is Ohio. It ain't Mississippi."

"White folks is white folks, honey, South or North, North or South," said Lucy Doves. "I's lived both places and I know."

"Yes, but in Mississippi they'd lynched Douglass by now."

"Where is Douglass?" asked Mattis Crane. "You all know I don't know much about this mess. Way back yonder on that farm where I lives, you don't get nothing straight. Where is Douglass?"

"Douglass is here! Saw him just now out in de field doin' his spring plowin' when I drive down de road, as stubborn and bold-faced as he can be. We told him he ought to leave here."

"Well, I wish he'd go on and get out," said Sister Wiggins. "If that would help any. His brother's got more sense than he has, even if he is a seventeen-year-old child. Clarence left here yesterday and went to Cleveland. But their ma, poor Sister Carter, she's still trying to battle it out. She told me last night, though, she thinks she have to leave. They won't let her have no more provisions at de general store. And they ain't got their spring seed yet. And they can't pay cash for 'em."

"Don't need to tell me! Old man Hartman's got evil as de rest of de white folks. Didn't he tell ma husband Saturday night he'd have to pay up every cent of his back bill, or he couldn't take nothing out of that store. And we been trading there for years."

"That's their way o' striking back at us niggers."

"Yes, but Lord knows my husband ain't de father o' that child."

"Nor mine."

"Jim's got too much pride to go foolin' round any old loose white woman."

"Child, you can't tell about men."

"I knowed a case once in Detroit where a nigger lived ten years with a white woman, and her husband didn't know it. He was their chauffeur."

"That's all right in the city, but please don't come bringing it out here to Boyd's Center where they ain't but a handful o' us colored—and we has a hard enough time as it is."

"You right! This sure has brought de hammer down on our heads."

"Lawd knows we's law-biding people, ain't harmed a soul, yet some o' these white folks talking 'bout trying to run all de colored folks out o' de country on account o' Douglass."

"They'll never run me," said Mrs. Sam Jones.

"Don't say what they *won't* do," said Lucy Doves, "cause they might."

"Howdy, Sister Jenkins."

"Howdy!"

"Good evenin'."

"Yes, de meetin' due to start directly."

"Soon as Madam President arrives. Reckon she's having trouble gettin' over that road from High Creek."

"Sit down and tell us what you's heard, Sister Jenkins."

"About Douglass?"

"Course 'bout Douglass. What else is anybody talkin' 'bout nowadays?"

"Well, my daughter told me Douglass' sister say they was in love."

"Him and that white woman?"

"Yes. Douglass' sister say it's been going on 'fore de woman got married."

"Un-huh! Then why didn't he stop foolin' with her after she got married? Bad enough, colored boy foolin' 'round a unmarried white woman, let alone a married one."

"Douglass' sister say they was in love."

"Well, why did she marry the *white* man, then?"

"She's white, ain't she? And who wouldn't marry a rich white man? Got his own farm, money and all, even if he were a widower with grown children gone to town. He give her everything she wanted, didn't he?"

"Everything but the right thing."

"Well, she must not o' loved him, sneaking 'round meeting Douglass in de woods."

"True."

"But what you reckon she went on and had that colored baby for?"

"She must a thought it was the old man's baby."

"She don't think so now! Mattie say when the doctor left and they brought the child in to show her, she like to went blind. It were near black as me."

"Do tell!"

"And what did her husband say?"

"Don't know. Don't know."

"He must a fainted."

"That old white woman lives across the crick from us said he's gonna put her out soon's she's able to walk."

"Ought to put her out!"

"Maybe that's what Douglass waitin' for."

"I heard he wants to take her away."

"He better take his fool self away, 'fore these white folks get madder. Ain't nobody heard it was a black baby till day before yesterday. Then it leaked out. And now de white folks are rarin' to kill Douglass!"

"I sure am scared!"

"And how come they all said right away it were Douglass?"

"Honey, don't you know? Colored folks knowed Douglass been eyeing that woman since God knows when, and she been eyeing back at him. You ought to seed 'em when they meet in de store. Course they didn't speak no more 'n Howdy, but their eyes followed one another 'round just like dogs."

"They was in love, I tell you. Been in love."

"Mighty funny kind o' love. Everybody knows can't no good come out o' white and colored love. Everybody knows that. And Douglass ain't no child. He's twenty-six years old, ain't he? And Sister Carter sure did try to raise her three chillun right. You can't blame her."

"Blame that fool boy, that's who, and that woman. Plenty colored girls in Camden he could of courted ten miles up de road. One or two right here. I got a daughter myself."

"No, he had to go foolin' round with a white woman."

"Yes, a white woman."

"They say he loved her."

"What do Douglass say, since it happened?"

"He don't say nothing."

"What could he say?"

"Well, he needn't think he's gonna keep his young mouth shut and let de white folks take it out on us. Down yonder at de school today, my Dorabella says they talkin' 'bout separatin' de colored from de white and makin' all de colored children go in a nigger room next term."

"Ain't nothing like that ever happened in Boyd's Center long as I been here—these twenty-two years."

"White folks is mad now, child, mad clean through."

"Wonder they ain't grabbed Douglass and lynched him."

"It's a wonder!"

"And him calmly out yonder plowin' de field this afternoon."

"He sure is brave."

"Woman's husband's liable to kill him."

"Her brother's done said he's gunning for him."

"They liable to burn Negroes' houses down."

"Anything's liable to happen. Lawd, I'm nervous as I can be."

"You can't tell about white folks."

"I ain't nervous. I'm *scared*."

"Don't say a word!"

"Why don't Sister Carter make him leave here?"

"I wish I knew."

"She told me she were nearly crazy."

"And she can't get Douglass to say nothin', one way or another—if he go, or if he stay. . . . Howdy, Madam President."

"Good evenin', Madam President."

"I done told you Douglass loves her."

"He wants to see that white woman, once more again, that's what he wants."

"A white hussy!"

"He's foolin' with fire."

"Poor Mis' Carter. I'm sorry for his mother."

"Poor Mis' Carter."

"Why don't you all say poor Douglass? Poor white woman? Poor child?"

"Madam President's startin' de meetin'."

"Is it boy or girl?"

"Sh-s-s-s! There's de bell."

"I hear it's a boy."

"Thank God, ain't a girl then."

"I hope it looks like Douglass, cause Douglass a fine-looking nigger."

"He's too bold, too bold."

"Shame he's got us all in this mess."

"Shame, shame, shame!"

"Sh-sss-sss!"

"Yes, indeedy!"

"Sisters, can't you hear this bell?"

"Shame!"

"Sh-sss!"

"Madam Secretary, take your chair."

"Shame!"

"The March meeting of the Salvation Rock Ladies' Missionary Society for the Rescue o' the African Heathen is hereby called to order. . . . Sister Burns, raise a hymn. . . . Will you-all ladies *please* be quiet? What are you talking 'bout back there anyhow?"

> *Ring a golden bell,*

"Heathens, daughter, heathens."

Aw, ring a golden bell,

"They ain't in Africa neither!"

Ring a golden bell for me.
Ring a golden bell,
Aw, ring a golden bell,
My Lawd's done set me free!

I was a sinner
Lost and lone,
Till Jesus claimed me
For His own.
Ring a golden bell,
Ring a golden bell,
Aw, ring a golden bell for me. . . .

ONE CHRISTMAS EVE

STANDING OVER THE HOT STOVE cooking supper, the colored maid, Arcie, was very tired. Between meals today, she had cleaned the whole house for the white family she worked for, getting ready for Christmas tomorrow. Now her back ached and her head felt faint from sheer fatigue. Well, she would be off in a little while, if only the Missus and her children would come on home to dinner. They were out shopping for more things for the tree which stood all ready, tinsel-hung and lovely in the living-room, waiting for its candles to be lighted.

Arcie wished she could afford a tree for Joe. He'd never had one yet, and it's nice to have such things when you're little. Joe was five, going on six. Arcie, looking at the roast in the white folks' oven, wondered how much she could afford to spend tonight on toys. She only got seven dollars a week, and four of that went for her room and the landlady's daily looking after Joe while Arcie was at work.

"Lord, it's more'n a notion raisin' a child," she thought.

She looked at the clock on the kitchen table. After seven. What made white folks so darned inconsiderate? Why didn't they come on home here to supper? They knew she wanted to get off before all the stores closed. She wouldn't have time to buy Joe nothin' if they didn't hurry. And her landlady probably wanting to go out and shop, too, and not be bothered with little Joe.

"Dog gone it!" Arcie said to herself. "If I just had my money, I might leave the supper on the stove for 'em. I just got to get to the stores fo' they close." But she hadn't been paid for the week yet. The Missus had promised to pay her Christmas Eve, a day or so ahead of time.

Arcie heard a door slam and talking and laughter in the front of the house. She went in and saw the Missus and her kids shaking snow off their coats.

"Umm-mm! It's swell for Christmas Eve," one of the kids said to Arcie. "It's snowin' like the deuce, and mother came near driving through a stop light. Can't hardly see for the snow. It's swell!"

"Supper's ready," Arcie said. She was thinking how her shoes weren't very good for walking in snow.

It seemed like the white folks took as long as they could to eat that evening. While Arcie was washing dishes, the Missus came out with her money.

"Arcie," the Missus said, "I'm so sorry, but would you mind if I just gave you five dollars tonight? The children have made me run short of change, buying presents and all."

"I'd like to have seven," Arcie said. "I needs it."

"Well, I just haven't got seven," the Missus said. "I didn't know you'd want all your money before the end of the week, anyhow. I just haven't got it to spare."

Arcie took five. Coming out of the hot kitchen, she wrapped up as well as she could and hurried by the house where she roomed to get little Joe. At least he could look at the Christmas trees in the windows downtown.

The landlady, a big light yellow woman, was in a bad humor. She said to Arcie, "I thought you was comin' home early and get this child. I guess you know I want to go out, too, once in awhile."

Arcie didn't say anything for, if she had, she knew the landlady would probably throw it up to her that she wasn't getting paid to look after a child both night and day.

"Come on, Joe," Arcie said to her son, "Let's us go in the street."

"I hears they got a Santa Claus down town," Joe said, wriggling into his worn little coat. "I wants to see him."

"Don't know 'bout that," his mother said, "but

hurry up and get your rubbers on. Stores'll all be closed directly."

It was six or eight blocks downtown. They trudged along through the falling snow, both of them a little cold. But the snow was pretty!

The main street was hung with bright red and blue lights. In front of the City Hall there was a Christmas tree—but it didn't have no presents on it, only lights. In the store windows there were lots of toys—for sale.

Joe kept on saying, "Mama, I want . . ."

But mama kept walking ahead. It was nearly ten, when the stores were due to close, and Arcie wanted to get Joe some cheap gloves and something to keep him warm, as well as a toy or two. She thought she might come across a rummage sale where they had children's clothes. And in the ten-cent store, she could get some toys.

"O-oo! Lookee . . .," little Joe kept saying, and pointing at things in the windows. How warm and pretty the lights were, and the shops, and the electric signs through the snow.

It took Arcie more than a dollar to get Joe's mittens and things he needed. In the A. & P. Arcie bought a big box of hard candies for 49c. And then she guided Joe through the crowd on the street until they came to the dime store. Near the ten-cent store they passed a moving picture theatre. Joe said he wanted to go in and see the movies.

Arcie said, "Ump-un! No, child! This ain't Balti-more where they have shows for colored, too. In these here small towns, they don't let colored folks in. We can't go in there."

"Oh," said little Joe.

In the ten-cent store, there was an awful crowd. Arcie told Joe to stand outside and wait for her. Keeping hold of him in the crowded store would be a job. Besides she didn't want him to see what toys she was buying. They were to be a surprise from Santa Claus tomorrow.

Little Joe stood outside the ten-cent store in the light, and the snow, and people passing. Gee, Christmas was pretty. All tinsel and stars and cot-ton. And Santa Claus a-coming from somewhere, dropping things in stockings. And all the people in the streets were carrying things, and the kids looked happy.

But Joe soon got tired of just standing and think-ing and waiting in front of the ten-cent store. There were so many things to look at in the other win-dows. He moved along up the block a little, and then a little more, walking and looking. In fact, he moved until he came to the white folks' picture show.

In the lobby of the moving picture show, behind the plate glass doors, it was all warm and glowing and awful pretty. Joe stood looking in, and as he looked his eyes began to make out, in there blazing beneath holly and colored streamers and the electric stars of the lobby, a marvellous Christmas tree. A group of children and grown-ups, white, of course, were standing around a big jovial man in red beside the tree. Or was it a man? Little Joe's eyes opened wide. No, it was not a man at all. It was Santa Claus!

Little Joe pushed open one of the glass doors and ran into the lobby of the white moving picture show. Little Joe went right through the crowd and up to where he could get a good look at Santa Claus. And Santa Claus was giving away gifts, little presents for children, little boxes of animal crackers and stick-candy canes. And behind him on the tree was a big sign (which little Joe didn't know how to read). It said, to those who understood, MERRY XMAS FROM SANTA CLAUS TO OUR YOUNG PATRONS.

Around the lobby, other signs said, WHEN YOU COME OUT OF THE SHOW STOP WITH YOUR CHILDREN AND SEE OUR SANTA CLAUS. And another announced, GEM THEATRE MAKES ITS CUSTOMERS HAPPY—SEE OUR SANTA.

And there was Santa Claus in a red suit and a white beard all sprinkled with tinsel snow. Around him were rattles and drums and rocking horses which he was not giving away. But the signs on them said (could little Joe have read) that they

would be presented from the stage on Christmas
Day to the holders of the lucky numbers. Tonight,
Santa Claus was only giving away candy, and stick-
candy canes, and animal crackers to the kids.

Joe would have liked terribly to have a stick-
candy cane. He came a little closer to Santa Claus,
until he was right in the front of the crowd. And
then Santa Claus saw Joe.

Why is it that lots of white people always grin
when they see a Negro child? Santa Claus grinned.
Everybody else grinned, too, looking at little black
Joe—who had no business in the lobby of a white
theatre. Then Santa Claus stooped down and slyly
picked up one of his lucky number rattles, a great
big loud tin-pan rattle such as they use in cabarets.
And he shook it fiercely right at Joe. That was
funny. The white people laughed, kids and all.
But little Joe didn't laugh. He was scared. To the
shaking of the big rattle, he turned and fled out of
the warm lobby of the theatre, out into the street
where the snow was and the people. Frightened by
laughter, he had begun to cry. He went looking for
his mama. In his heart he never thought Santa
Claus shook great rattles at children like that—and
then laughed.

In the crowd on the street he went the wrong
way. He couldn't find the ten-cent store or his
mother. There were too many people, all white

people, moving like white shadows in the snow, a world of white people.

It seemed to Joe an awfully long time till he suddenly saw Arcie, dark and worried-looking, cut across the side-walk through the passing crowd and grab him. Although her arms were full of packages, she still managed with one free hand to shake him until his teeth rattled.

"Why didn't you stand where I left you?" Arcie demanded loudly. "Tired as I am, I got to run all over the streets in the night lookin' for you. I'm a great mind to wear you out."

When little Joe got his breath back, on the way home, he told his mama he had been in the moving picture show.

"But Santa Claus didn't give me nothin'," Joe said tearfully. "He made a big noise at me and I runned out."

"Serves you right," said Arcie, trudging through the snow. "You had no business in there. I told you to stay where I left you."

"But I seed Santa Claus in there," little Joe said, "so I went in.'

"Huh! That wasn't no Santa Claus," Arcie explained. "If it was, he wouldn't a-treated you like that. That's a theatre for white folks—I told you once—and he's just a old white man."

"Oh . . .," said little Joe.

FATHER AND SON

COLONEL THOMAS NORWOOD STOOD in his doorway at the Big House looking down the dusty plantation road. Today his youngest son was coming home. A heavy Georgia spring filled the morning air with sunshine and earth-perfumes. It made the old man feel strangely young again. Bert was coming home.

Twenty years ago he had begotten him.

This boy, however, was not his real son, for Colonel Thomas Norwood had no real son, no white and legal heir to carry on the Norwood name; this boy was a son by his Negro mistress, Coralee Lewis, who kept his house and had borne him all his children.

Colonel Norwood never would have admitted, even to himself, that he was standing in his doorway waiting for this half-Negro son to come home. But in truth that is what he was doing. He was curious about this boy. How would he look after all these years away at school? Six or seven surely, for not once in that long time had he been allowed to come back to Big House Plantation. The Colonel had said then that never did he want to see the boy.

But in truth he did—for this boy had been, after all, the most beautiful of the lot, the brightest and the badest of the Colonel's five children, lording it over the other children, and sassing not only his colored mother, but his white father, as well. Handsome and mischievous, favoring too much the Colonel in looks and ways, this boy Bert, at fourteen, had got himself sent off to school to stay. Now a student in college (or what they call a college in Negro terms in Georgia) he was coming home for the summer vacation.

Today his brother, Willie, had been sent to the station to meet him in the new Ford. The ten o'clock train must have reached the Junction by now, thought the Colonel, standing in the door. Soon the Ford would be shooting back down the road in a cloud of dust, curving past the tall white pillars of the front porch, and around to the kitchen stoop where Cora would greet her child.

Thinking thus, Colonel Norwood came inside the house, closed the screen, and pulled at a bell-cord hanging from the wall of the great dark living-room with its dignified but shabby horse hair furniture of the nineties. By and by, an old Negro serv-ant, whose name was Sam and who wore a kind of old-fashioned butler's coat, came and brought the Colonel a drink.

"I'm going in my library where I don't want to be disturbed."

"Yes, suh," said the Negro servant.

"You hear me?"

"Yes, suh," said the servant, knowing that when Colonel Norwood said "library", he meant he did not want to be disturbed.

The Colonel entered the small room where he kept his books and papers of both a literary and a business nature. He closed the door. He did this deliberately, intending to let all the Negroes in the house know that he had no interest whatsoever in the homecoming about to take place. He intended to remain in the library several hours after Bert's arrival. Yet, as he bent over his desk peering at accounts his store-keeper had brought him, his head kept turning toward the window that gave on the yard and the road, kept looking to see if a car were coming in a cloud of dust.

An hour or so later, when shouts of welcome, loud warm Negro-cries, laughter, and the blowing of an auto horn filled the Georgia sunlight outside, the Colonel bent more closely over his ledgers—but he did turn his eyes a little to catch the dust sifting in the sunny air above the road where the car had passed. And his mind went back to that little olive-colored kid he had beaten one day in the stables years ago—the kid grown up now, and just come home.

He had always been a little ashamed of that

particular beating he had given the boy. But his temper had got the best of him. That child, Bert, looking almost like a white child (a hell of a lot favoring the Colonel), had come running out to the stables one afternoon when he was showing his horses to some guests from in town. The boy had come up to him crying, "Papa!" (He knew better, right in front of company.) "Papa, Ma says she's got dinner ready."

The Colonel had knocked him down under the feet of the horses right there in front of the guests. And afterwards he had locked him in the stable and beaten him severely. The boy had to learn not to call him papa, and certainly not in front of white people from the town.

But it had been hard to teach Bert anything, the Colonel ruminated. Trouble was, the boy was too smart. There were other unpleasant memories of that same saucy ivory-skinned youngster playing about the front yard, even running through the Big House, in spite of orders that Coralee's children and all other pickaninnies keep to the back of the house, or down in the Quarters. But as a child, Bert had never learned his place.

"He's too damn much like me," the Colonel thought. "Quick as hell. Cora's been telling me he's leading his class at the Institute, and a football captain. . . . H-m-m-m, so they waste their time playing football at these darkie colleges. . . . Well, anyway, he must be a smart darkie. Got my blood in him."

The Colonel had Sam bring some food into the library. He pretended to be extremely busy, and did not give the old Negro, bursting with news, a chance to speak. The Colonel acted as though he were unaware of the presence of the newly arrived boy on the plantation; or if he were aware, completely uninterested, and completely occupied.

But in the late afternoon, the Colonel got up from his desk, went out into the parlor, picked up an old straw hat, and strolled through the front door, across the wide-porticoed porch with its white pillars, and down the road toward the South Field. The Colonel saw the brown backs of his Negroes in the green cotton. He smelt the earth-scent of a day that had been long and hot. He turned off by the edge of a field, went down to the creek, and back toward the house along a path that took him through a grove of pecan trees skirting the old slave quarters, to the back door of the Big House.

Long before he approached the Big House, he could hear Negroes' voices, musical and laughing. Then he could see a small group of dark bare arms and faces about the kitchen stoop. Cora was sitting on a stool in the yard, probably washing fruit for jelly. Livonia, the fat old cook, was on the porch shelling peas for dinner. Seated on the stoop, and on the ground, and standing around, were colored persons the Colonel knew had no good reason to be there at that time of day. Some of them, when they saw the Colonel coming, began to move away, back toward the barns, or whatever work they were doing.

He was aware, too, standing in the midst of this group, of a tall young man in sporty white trousers, black-and-white oxfords, and a blue shirt. He looked very clean and well-dressed, like a white man. The Colonel took this to be his son, and a certain vibration shook him from head to foot. Across the wide dusty yard, their eyes met. The Colonel's brows came together, his shoulders lifted and went back as though faced by an indignity just suffered. His chin went up. And he began to think, on the way toward them, how he would walk through this group like a white man. The Negroes, of course, would be respectful and afraid, as usual. He would say merely, "Good evening, Bert," to this boy, his son, then wait a moment, perhaps, and see what the boy said before passing on into the house.

Laughter died and dripped and trickled away, and talk quieted, and silence fell degree by degree, each step the white man approached. A strange sort of stiffness like steel nearing steel grew and straightened between the colored boy in the black-and-white shoes and the old Colonel who had just come from looking at his fields and his Negroes working.

"Good evening, Bert," the Colonel said.

"Good evening, Colonel Tom," the boy replied quickly, politely, almost eagerly. And then, like a puppet pulled by some perverse string, the boy offered his hand.

The Colonel looked at the strong young near-white hand held out toward him, and made no effort to take it. His eyes lifted to the eyes of the boy, his son, in front of him. The boy's eyes did not fall. But a slow flush reddened the olive of his skin as the old man turned without a word toward the stoop and into the house. The boy's hand went to his side again. A hum of dark voices broke the silence.

This happened between father and son. The mother sitting there washing plums in a pail, did not understand what had happened. But the water from which she took the plums felt cool to her hands that were suddenly burning hot.

II

Coralee Lewis, sitting washing plums, had been Colonel Norwood's mistress for thirty years. She had lived in the Big House, supervised his life, given him children, and loved him. In his turn, he felt something very like love for her. Now, in his sixties, without Cora he would have been lost, but of course he did not realize that—consciously.

The history of their liaison, like that of so many between Negro women and white men in the South, began without love, at least on his part. For a long while its motif was lust—whose sweeter name, perhaps, is passion.

The Colonel had really known Cora all her life. As a half-grown boy, he had teased her as a baby, pulling her kinky braids and laughing at the way she rolled in the dust with the other pickaninnies born to the black servants and share-croppers on his father's plantation. He had seen her as a girl, barefooted and shy, brown face shining, bringing milk to the Big House night and morning, for her father took care of the cows. Her mother worked sometimes in the house but mostly in the fields. And Cora knew early how to pick cotton, too.

Then there came years when young Norwood had no contact with Cora: years when he had been away at Military School; those first few years when he had come back from Macon with his new bride; those years of love and worry with the delicate and lovely woman he had wedded. During his early married life the Colonel could not truthfully remember ever having laid eyes on Cora, although she was about the place surely.

But Cora remembered often seeing the Colonel. Young and handsome, tall and straight, he drove over the plantation roads with the wisp of a pretty little lady he had married. She remembered him particularly well the day of his father's funeral, when he came back from the burial—he and his wife, master and mistress of the Big House now. How sad and worried young Colonel Norwood looked that day descending from the carriage.

And as the months went by, he began to look more and more worried and weary. Servants' gossip from the Big House, drifting down to the humbler Negroes in the cabins, said that a wall had grown up between the young Colonel and his little wife, who seemed to be wasting away day by day. A wall like a mist. And the Negroes began to laugh that there were never no children born to Mister and Missus. Then gossip began to say that the young Colonel had taken up with the cook's daughter, black but comely Livonia, who worked in the pantry. Then the Quarters laughed all the more—for Livonia had four or five Negro lovers, too. And she wasn't faithful to anybody—just liked to love.

Cora heard all this and in her mind a certain envy sprang up. Livonia! Huh! Cora began to look more carefully into the cracked mirror in her mother's cabin. She combed her hair and oiled it better than before. She was seventeen then.

"Time you was takin' some pride about yo'self," said her mother, noting the change.

"Yes'm," said Cora. And when she took milk to the Big House now, she tried to look her best.

One night, there was a party there. A great many people came from the Junction, and even seventy miles off from in town, by horse and by carriage, by train, and even some by that new-fangled auto-buggy that most of the plantation hands had never seen before. The Negroes were all excited at having so many white folks around. It was the Missus' birthday. There were great doings at Big House Plantation.

The first evening, the party went on until late in the night. Some people left at dawn. Others slept awhile and left in the afternoon. Some were house guests, and on the second night there was a party again. But that night everybody was pretty tired. And got pretty drunk, too, mostly. The Colonel was very gay and very drunk; but his little wife cried, and went to bed. She was mighty touchy, all the Negroes knew. Always poutin' and spattin' and actin' funny with the Colonel.

Wonder why? Wonder why?

There was a party in the Quarters among the Negroes, too, that second night. Livonia was there, dancing fit to kill. And the music was wild. In the heat of the night, Cora went out of the barn where the party was, out into the moonlight, and looked up at the lights of the Big House on the rise. She stretched, and breathed in the warm night air, and walked through the trees toward the road that ran to town. She made a big circle about the Big House, wondering a little what was going on there. When she got to the road, she sat down under a huge live oak tree. She could hear the laughter and clapping of the Negroes down on the edge of the cotton fields. But in the Big House, where it should have been gay, too, it was mighty quiet. Sometimes a loud and quarrelsome voice could be heard. Probably the men were gambling, and the ladies gone to bed.

The trees cast great shadows across the road in the warm light of the moon. Cora stretched, breathed deeply again, and got up to go, when she saw very near her a figure walking in the silvery dusk, a tall thin young white man walking in the cotton. Suddenly he called her.

"Who're you?" It was young Norwood speaking.

"I's Coralee Lewis, Aunt Tobie Lewis' daughter."

The white man came up to her, took her brown face in his hands and lifted it at the moon. "You're out mighty late," he said.

Cora's body trembled. Her mouth opened. In the shadow of the live oak tree there by the road, thirty years ago, in a night of moon. . . .

III

When the first child, Willie, was in her, she told her mother all about it. The old woman was glad.

"It's better'n slavin' in the cotton fields," she said. "I's known colored women what's wore silk dresses and lived like queens on plantations right here in Georgy. . . ."

Even before the young Mrs. Norwood died (she did die—and childless) Cora was working in the Big House. And after Mrs. Norwood's death, Cora came there to sleep.

Now the water where the plums were felt cool to her hands this spring afternoon many years later as the Colonel went into the house leaving their youngest boy dazed in front of her; and the nigger-voices all around her humming and chattering into loudness and laughter.

IV

"Listen hyar," brother Willie said to Bert on the way from the Junction to the plantation that morning his brother arrived. "Listen hyar, I hopes you don't expect to go around all dressed up like you is now after you gets out to de place, 'cause de Colonel won't 'low it. He made Sis put away all them fine clothes she brought hyar last year—till she left."

"Tell him to kiss my behind," Bert said.

Willie bucked his eyes, stuttered, then kept quiet. His brother was the same Bert as he had been as a child. Crazy! Trouble coming. William made up his mind not to be in it, himself, one way or another. Though he was eight years older, he had always been afraid of Bert with a fear worse than physical, afraid of the things that happened around Bert.

From the new Ford, Bert looked out at the straggling streets of the village of the Junction, at the Negroes lounging in front of stores, at the red-necked crackers, at the unkempt women. He heard the departing train whistle as it went deeper into Georgia, into Alabama. As they rode, he looked at the wide fields of young cotton stretching on either side, at the cabins of the share croppers, at the occasional house of a white owner or overseer. Then he saw the gradual rise of the Norwood plantation, the famous Big House, surrounded by its live oaks and magnolias and maples, and its many acres of cotton. And he knew he was nearing home.

Six years away. Kid of fourteen when he left, wearing his first long trousers bought in the commissary store, feeling funny out of overalls, feeling very proud going away to school. Only the Lewis niggers (old man Norwood's kids by Cora) went away to school in these parts. And with the going of Sallie, the youngest, the little county school at Norwood's Crossroads closed up, and didn't open any more. Sallie was the *Colonel's* last child—no other niggers needed a school.

Old Aunt Tobie, the grandma, before she died, used to keep on saying that the Lewis young 'uns ought to appreciate what the Colonel was doing for 'em. No white man she ever heard of cared anything 'bout educatin' his tar-brush chillun. But the Colonel did. Somehow 'nother Cora was able to put it in the Colonel's mind and keep it there until the last child, Sallie, got sent off to Atlanta.

In Atlanta, Bert had entered the same run-down Negro boarding school, the Institute, that brother Willie and his oldest sister, Bertha, had attended. But Willie, several years before, hadn't stayed there long, being a dumb boy who liked the plantation better. Bertha had gone up North once with the Spiritual Jubilee Singers, and liked it so well that she remained to work in Chicago. Now, little sister Sallie, seventeen, went to the Institute also, but had come home this spring ahead of Bert, who fooled around Atlanta a week or so before leaving, not wanting to come home really.

"Home, hell!"

Bert didn't want to come home. He felt he had no home. A brown mother, and a white father; bed for him in a nigger cabin down on the edge of the cotton fields. Soon as Cora's kids stopped nursing they went to live outside the Big House. Aunt Tobie, the grandmother, had really raised them, until she died. Then a cousin of Cora's brought up Sallie.

"Hell of a way to live," Bert thought, the night before his arrival, sitting in the Jim Crow car bound for south Georgia. During the long ride, he had turned over in his mind incidents of his childhood on the Big House Plantation. Sitting in the smoky half-coach allotted to Negroes (the other half being a baggage car) he thought of what it meant growing up as one of Colonel Norwood's yard-niggers (a term used by field hands for the mulatto children of a white planter).

"It's hell," Bert thought.

Not that Cora's other kids had found it hell. Only he had found it so, strangely enough. "The rest of 'em are too dumb, except little Sallie, and she don't say nothing—but it's hell to her, too, I reckon," the boy thought to himself as the train rocked and rumbled over the road. "Willie don't give a damn so long as his belly's full. And Bertha's got up North away from it all. I don't know what she really thought. . . . But I wish it hadn't happened to me."

With the self-pity of bewildered youth, he began to think about himself. Always, he had known the Colonel was his father, from the earliest he could remember. For one thing, Bert had been lighter than any of the other colored children on the plantation—a sort of ivory white. And as a small child, his hair had been straight and brown, his eyes grey, like Norwood's. His grandma, old Aunt Tobie, used to refer to them all, Willie and Bertha and Bert and Sallie, not without pride, as Colonel

Tom's children. (There had been another brother who died.) Bert noticed early in life that all the other kids in the Quarters were named after their fathers, whereas he and his brother and sisters bore the mother's name, Lewis. He was Bert Lewis—not Bert Norwood. His mother slept in the Big House —but the children lived outside with Aunt Tobie or Cousin Betty. Those things puzzled little Bert.

As he grew up, he used to hear folks remarking on how much he looked like Colonel Tom, and how little like Cora. Nearly light enough to pass for white, folks said, spittin' image of his father, too. Bert had a temper and ways like white folks, too. Indeed, "You needn't act so much like quality with me," was one of Aunt Tobie's favorite ways of reprimanding him when she wanted to take him down a peg or two.

He was always getting into mischief, playing pranks and worrying his mother at the backdoor of the Big House. There was a time once when the Colonel seemed to get pleasure out of letting little Bert trail around at his heels, but that period didn't last very long, for young Bert sassed the Colonel, too, just as though he were colored. And somehow, he had acquired that way of referring to Norwood as papa. The Colonel told him, sternly and seriously, "Boy, don't *you* use that word to me." But still, forgetful little devil that he was, he had come running up to the Colonel that day in the stables yelling, "Papa, dinner's ready."

The slap that he received made him see stars and darkness, Bert remembered. As though he were brushing a fly out of the way, the Colonel had knocked him down under the feet of the horses, and went on talking to his guests. After the guests had gone, he switched Bert mercilessly.

Can't nobody teach you nothin' but a switch, nohow," said old Aunt Tobie afterwards. "I tole you 'bout gittin' familiar wid that white man."

"But he didn't need to scar him all up," Bert remembered Cora's saying when she saw the black and blue marks on his back. "I ain't bearin' him children for to beat 'em to death. . . . You stay way from him, son, you hear?"

From that time on, between Bert and the Colonel, there had been a barrier of fear—a fear that held a certain mysterious fascination for Bert's sense of defiance, a fear that Bert from afar was continually taunting and baiting. For instance, the Colonel had a complex, Bert recalled, that all the Negroes knew, about the front door of the Big House. His orders were that no Negroes go in and out of that door, or cross his front porch. When the old house-man, Sam, wanted to sweep off the porch, he would have to go out the back and come all the way around. It was as absurd as that. Yet Bert, as a child, in the Big House visiting or helping Cora, would often dart out the front way when he thought the Colonel was in town or down in the South Field, or asleep in his library. Cora used to spank him for it, but it was a habit he kept up until he went away, a big boy, to Atlanta.

Bert, home-bound now, smiled to himself in the stuffy Jim Crow car, and wondered if the Colonel were still as tall and stern and stiff fronted as he used to be. No wonder his young white wife had died years ago—having to live with him—although, according to Aunt Tobie's version, the Colonel had humored her in every way. He really loved her, folks said, and had sworn after her death that he would never marry again. He hadn't—he had taken Cora.

And here Bert's mind balked and veered away from speculating about the intimate life of this old man and his mother. Bert knew that in a sense the white man had been kind to her. He remembered as a child the extra little delicacies that came down to Aunt Tobie and Cousin Betty and Cora's other relatives in the Quarters, especially at Christmas. He remembered how he had always known that the little colored school had not been there before Cora's children were born, and that it was no longer at the Cross Roads now. (For the Colonel and Mr. Higgins, being political powers in the county, were in charge of education, and their policy was to let Negroes remain unlettered. They worked better.) Bert knew, too, that it was his mother's influence that had got her children sent off to the Institute in Atlanta. But it was the *Colonel's* dislike of Bert that had kept him there, summer and winter, until now. Not that Bert minded. Summer school was fun, too. And tennis. And the pleasures of the town. And he was never homesick for the plantation—but he did wish sometimes that he had a home, and that the Colonel would treat him like a son.

Tall and light and good-looking, as Bert was now at twenty, he could have a very good time in Atlanta. Colored society had taken him up. He went around with the sons and daughters of Negro doctors and dentists and insurance brokers and professors. He had his hands full of pretty girls. Lots of cream-colored girls, chocolate brown girls, velvet-soft night-shade girls all liked Bert. And already he had been involved in a scandal with a doctor's wife.

To add to his good looks, Bert was an excellent athlete. He had been as far north as Washington with Institute teams, and had seen colored people at the Capitol riding in street cars where there had been no Jim Crow signs, and getting on trains that had no coaches especially for Negroes. Bert made up his mind to come North to live, as soon as he finished school. He had one more year. And this last summer, Cora wanted him to spend with her—because she sensed he might never come back to the plantation again.

Sallie, his sister, three classes behind him at the Institute, was frankly worried about his going home. She was afraid. "Colonel Tom's getting old. He ain't nice a-tall like he kinder used to be. He's getting more and more touchy," Sallie said to her brother. "And I know he ain't gonna like the looks of you. You don't look a bit like a Georgia boy any more."

"To hell with him," said Bert.

"I wouldn't even know you and Willie were brothers," Sallie said. For Sallie went home every summer and worked in the Big House with her mother, and saw Willie, and knew how things were on the plantation. Willie and the Colonel got along fine, because Willie was docile and good-natured and nigger-like, bowing and scraping and treating white folks like they expected to be treated. "But Bert, you ain't a bit like that."

"Why should I be?" Bert asked. "I'm the old man's son, ain't I? Got white blood in me, too."

"Yes, but . . ."

"But what?" Bert said. "Let old knotty-headed Willie go on being a white-folks' nigger if he wants to, I won't!"

And that's the way it was when he came home.

v

There are people (you've probably noted it also) who have the unconscious faculty of making the world spin around themselves, throb and expand, contract and go dizzy. Then, when they are gone away, you feel sick and lonesome and meaningless.

In the chemistry lab at school, did you ever hold a test tube, pouring in liquids and powders and seeing nothing happen until a *certain* liquid or a *certain* powder is poured in and then everything begins to smoke and fume, bubble and boil, hiss to foam, and sometimes even explode? The tube is suddenly full of action and movement and life. Well, there are people like those certain liquids or powders; at a given moment they come into a room, or into a town, even into a country—and the place is never the same again. Things bubble, boil, change. Sometimes the whole world is changed. Alexander came. Christ. Marconi. A Russian named Lenin.

Not that there is any comparing Bert to Christ or Lenin. But after he returned to the Big House Plantation that summer, life was never the same. From Bert's very first day on the place something was broken, something went dizzy. The world began to spin, to ferment, and move into a new action.

Not to be a *white folks' nigger*—Bert had come home with that idea in his head.

The Colonel sensed it in his out-stretched hand and his tall young body—and had turned his back and walked into the house. Cora with her hands in the cool water where the plums were, suddenly knew in her innermost soul a period of time had closed for her. That first night she prayed, cried in her room, asked the Lord why she had ever let her son come home. In his cabin Willie prayed, too, humble, Lord, humble. The Colonel rocked alone on his front porch sucking a black cigar and cussing bitterly at he knew not what. The hum and laughter of the Negro voices went on as usual on the vast plantation down to the last share-cropper's cabin, but not quite, not *quite* the same as they had been in the morning. And never to be the same again.

"Is you heard about Bert?"

Not to be a *white folks' nigger!*

Bow down and pray in fear and trembling, go way back in the dark afraid; or work harder and harder; or stumble and learn; or raise up your fist and strike—but once the idea comes into your head you'll never be the same again. Oh, test tube of life! Crucible of the South, find the right powder and you'll never be the same again—the cotton will blaze and the cabins will burn and the chains will be broken and men, all of a sudden, will shake hands, black men and white men, like steel meeting steel!

"The bastard," Bert said. "Why couldn't he shake hands with me? I'm a Norwood, too."

"Hush, son," said Cora with the cool water from the plums on her hands.

And the hum of the black voices that afternoon spread to the cabins, to the cotton fields, to the dark streets of the Junction, what Bert had said—Bert with the ivory-yellow skin and the tall proud young body, Bert come home not to be a white folks' nigger.

"Lawd, chile, Bert's come home. . . ."

"Lawd, chile, and he said . . ."

"Lawd, chile, he said . . ."

"Lawd, chile . . ."

"Lawd . . ."

VI

July passed, and August. The hot summer sun marched across the skies. The Colonel ordered Bert to work in the fields. Bert had not done so. Talbot, the white foreman, washed his hands of it, saying that if he had his way, "that nigger would be run off the place."

For the Colonel, the summer was hectic enough,

what with cotton prices dropping on the market; share-croppers restless and moving; one black field-hand beaten half to death by Talbot and the store-keeper because he "talked high" to a neighboring white planter; news of the Scottsboro trials and the Camp Hill shootings exciting black labor.

Colonel Norwood ordered the colored rural Baptist minister to start a revival and keep it going until he said stop. Let the Negroes sing and shout their troubles away, as in the past. White folks had always found revivals a useful outlet for sullen over-worked darkies. As long as they were singing and praying, they forgot about the troubles of this world. In a frenzy of rhythm and religion, they laid their cross at the feet of Jesus.

Poor over-worked Jesus! Somehow since the War, he hadn't borne that cross so well. Too heavy, it's too heavy! Lately, Negroes seem to sense that it's not Jesus' cross, anyhow, it's their own. Only old people praise King Jesus any more. On the Nor-wood plantation, Bert's done told the young people to stop being white folks' niggers. More and more, the Colonel felt it was Bert who brought trouble into the Georgia summer. The revival was a failure.

One day he met the boy coming back from the river where he had been swimming. The Colonel lit into him with all the cuss words at his command. He told him in no uncertain language to get down in the South Field to work. He told him there would be no more school at Atlanta for him; that he would show him that just because Cora happened to be his mother, he was no more than any other nigger on the place. God damn him!

Bert stood silent and red in front of his father, looking as the Colonel must have looked forty years ago—except that he was a shade darker. He did not go down to the South Field to work. And all Cora's pleadings could not make him go. Yet nothing happened. That was the strange thing about it. The Colonel did nothing—to Bert. But he lit into Cora, nagged and scolded her for days, told her she'd better get some sense into her boy's head if she wanted any skin left on his body.

So the summer passed. Sallie, having worked faithfully in the house throughout the hottest months, went away to school again. Bert remained sullenly behind.

The day that ends our story began like this:

The sun rose burning and blazing, flooding the earth with the heat of early autumn, making even the morning oppressive. Folks got out of bed feeling like over-ripe fruit. The air of the morning shimmered with heat and ill-humor. The night before, Colonel Norwood had been drinking. He got up trembling and shaky, yelling for Cora to bring him something clean to put on. He went downstairs cussing.

The Colonel did not want to eat. He drank black

coffee, and walked out on the tall-pillared porch
to get a breath of air. He was standing there looking through the trees at his cotton, when the Ford
swept by in a cloud of dust, past the front of the
house and down the highway to town. Bert was
driving.

The Colonel cussed out loud, bit his cigar,
turned and went into the house, slamming the door,
storming to Cora, calling up the stairs where she was
working, "What the hell does he think he is, driving off to town in the middle of the morning?
Didn't I tell Bert not to touch that Ford, to stay
down yonder in the fields and work?"

"Yes, suh, Colonel Tom," Cora said. "You sure
did."

"Tell him I want to see him soon as he comes
back here. Send him in here. And tell him I'll skin
his yellow hide for him." The Colonel spoke of
Bert as though he were still a child.

"Yes, suh, Colonel Tom."

VII

The day grew hotter and hotter. Heat waves rose
from the fields. Sweat dampened the Colonel's
body. Sweat dampened the black bodies of the Negroes in the cotton fields, too, the hard black bodies that had built the Colonel's fortune out of earth
and sun and barehanded labor. Yet the Colonel, in

spite of the fact that he lived on this labor, sat in his shaded house fanning that morning and wondering what made niggers so contrary—he was thinking of Bert—as the telephone rang. The fat and testy voice of his old friend, Mr. Higgins, trembled at the other end of the wire. He was calling from the Junction.

Accustomed as he was to his friend's voice on the phone, at first the Colonel could not make out what he was saying. When he did understand, his neck bulged and the palms of the hands that held the phone were wet with sweat. Anger and shame made his tall body stoop and bend like an animal about to spring. Mr. Higgins was talking about Bert.

"That yellow nigger . . ." Mr. Higgins said. "One of your yard-niggers sassed . . ." Mr. Higgins said. "I thought I'd better tell you . . ." Mr. Higgins said. "Everybody . . ." Mr. Higgins said.

The whole town was excited about Bert. In the heat of this over-warm autumn day, the hot heads of the white citizens of the town had suddenly become inflamed about Bert. Mr. Higgins, county politician and Postmaster at the Junction, was well qualified to know. His Office had been the center of the news.

It seemed that Bert had insulted the young white woman who sold stamps and made out money-orders at the Post Office. And Mr. Higgins was telling the Colonel about it on the phone, warning him to get rid of Bert, that people around the Junction were getting sick and tired of seeing him.

At the Post Office this is what happened: a simple argument over change. But the young woman who sold the stamps was not used to arguing with Negroes, or being corrected by them when she made a mistake. Bert said, "I gave you a dollar," holding out the incorrect change. "You gave me back only sixty-four cents."

The young woman said, counting the change, "Yes, but you have eight three-cent stamps. Move on now, there're others waiting." Several white people were in line.

Bert said, "Yes, but eight times three is not thirty-six. You owe me twelve cents more."

The girl looked at the change and realized she was wrong. She looked at Bert—light near-white nigger with grey-blue eyes. You gotta be harder on those kind than you have on the black ones. An educated nigger, too! Besides it was hot and she wasn't feeling well. A light near-white nigger with grey eyes! Instead of correcting the change, she screamed, and let her head fall forward in front of the window.

Two or three white men waiting to buy stamps seized Bert and attempted to throw him out of the Post Office. Bert remembered he'd been a football player—and Colonel Norwood's son—so he fought back. One of the white men got a bloody mouth. Women screamed. Bert walked out of the Post Office, got in the Ford and drove away. By that time, the girl who sold stamps had recovered. She was telling everyone how Bert had insulted her.

"Oh, my God! It was terrible," she said.

"That's one nigger don't know his place, Tom," Mr. Higgins roared over the phone. "And it's your fault he don't—sendin' 'em off to school to be educated." The Colonel listened to his friend at the other end of the wire. "Why that yellow buck comes to my store and if he ain't waited on quick as the white folks are, he walks out. He said last week standin' out on my corner, he wasn't *all* nigger no how; said his name was Norwood—not Lewis, like the rest of Cora's family; said your plantation would be his when you passed out—and all that kind o' stuff, boasting to the niggers listening about you being his father." The Colonel almost dropped the phone. "Now, Tom, you know that stuff don't go 'round these parts o' Georgia. Ruinous to other niggers hearing that sort of talk, too. There ain't been no race trouble in our county for three years —since the Deekins lynching—but I'm telling you, Norwood, folks ain't gonna stand for this. I'm speaking on the quiet, but I see ahead. What happened this morning in the Post Office ain't none too good."

"When I get through with him," said the Colonel hoarsely, "you won't need to worry. Goodbye."

The white man came out of the library, yelled for Sam, shouted for Cora, ordered whisky. Drank and screamed.

"God damn that son of yours! I'm gonna kill him," he said to Cora. "Get out of here," he shouted at Sam, who came back with cigars.

Cora wept. The Colonel raved. A car shot down the road. The Colonel rushed out, brandishing a cane to stop it. It was Bert. He paid no attention to the old man standing on the steps of the pillared porch waving his stick. Ashen with fury, the Colonel came back into the house and fumbled with his keys at an old chest. Finally, a drawer opened and he took out a pistol. He went toward the door as Cora began to howl, but on the porch he became suddenly strengthless and limp. Shaking, the old man sank into a chair holding the gun. He would not speak to Cora.

VIII

Late in the afternoon, Colonel Norwood sent Cora for their son. The gun had been put away. At least Cora did not see it.

"I want to talk to that boy," the Colonel said. "Fetch him here." Damned young fool . . . bastard . . . of a nigger. . . .

"What's he gonna do to my boy?" Cora thought.

"Son, be careful," as she went across the yard and down toward Willie's cabin to find Bert. "Son, you be careful. I didn't bear you for no white man to kill. Son, you be careful. You ain't white, don't you know that? You be careful. O, Lord God Jesus in heaven! Son, be careful!" Cora was crying when she reached Willie's door, crying all the way back to the Big House with her son.

"To hell with the old man," Bert said. "He ain't no trouble! Old as he is, what can he do to me?"

"Lord have mercy, son, is you crazy? Why don't you be like Willie? He ain't never had no fusses with de Colonel."

"White folks' nigger," Bert said.

"Why don't you talk sense?" Cora begged.

"Why didn't he keep his promise then and let me go back to school in Atlanta, like my sister? You said if I came home this summer he'd lemme go back to the Institute, didn't you? Then why didn't he?"

"Why didn't you act right, son? Oh-o-o!" Cora moaned. "You can't get nothin' from white folks if you don't act right."

"Act like Willie, you mean, and the rest of these cotton pickers? Then I don't want anything."

They had reached the back door now. It was nearly dark in the kitchen where Livonia was making biscuits.

"Don't rile him, Bert, child," Cora said as she

took him through the house. "I don't know what he might do to you. He's got a gun."

"Don't worry 'bout me," Bert answered.

The setting sun made long paths of golden light across the parlor floor through the tall windows opening on the West. The air was thick and sultry with autumn heat. The Colonel sat, bent and old, near a table where there were whisky and cigars and a half-open drawer. When Bert entered he suddenly straightened up and the old commanding look came into his eyes. He told Cora to go upstairs to her room.

Of course, he never asked Bert to sit down.

The tall mulatto boy stood before his father, the Colonel. The old white man felt the steel of him standing there, like the steel of himself forty years ago. Steel of the Norwoods darkened now by Africa. The old man got up, straight and tall, too, and suddenly shook his fist in the face of the boy.

"You listen to me," he said, trembling with quiet. "I don't want to have to whip you again like I did when you were a child." He was almost hissing. "The next time I might kill you. I been running this plantation thirty-five years and never had to beat a nigger old as you are. Never had any trouble out of none of Cora's children before either, but you." The old man sat down. "I don't have trouble with my colored folks. They do what I say or what Talbot says, and that's all there is to it. If they turn in crops, they get a living. If they work for wages, they get paid. If they spend their money on licker, or old cars, or fixing up their cabins—they can do what they choose, long as they know their places and it don't hinder their work. To Cora's young ones—you hear me, boy?—I gave all the chances any nigger ever had in these parts. More'n many a white child's had, too. I sent you off to school. I gave your brother, Willie, that house he's living in when he got married, pay him for his work, help him out if he needs it. None of my darkies suffer. You went off to school. Could have kept on, would have sent you back this fall, but I don't intend to pay for no nigger, or white boy either if I had one, that acts the way you been acting." Colonel Norwood got up again, angrily. "And certainly not for no black fool! I'm talking to *you* like this only because you're Cora's child—but you know damn well it's my habit to *tell* people what to do, not discuss it with them. I just want to know what's the matter with you, though—whether you're crazy or not? And if you're not, you'd better change your ways a damn sight or it won't be safe for you here, and you know it—venting your impudence on white women, ruining my niggers, driving like mad through the Junction, carrying on just as you please. I'm warning you, boy, God damn it! . . . Now I want you to answer me, and talk right."

The old man sat down in his chair again by the whisky bottle and the partly opened drawer. He took a drink.

"What do you mean, talk right?" Bert said.

"I mean talk like a nigger should to a white man," the Colonel snapped.

"Oh, but I'm not a nigger, Colonel Norwood," Bert said, "I'm your son."

The old man frowned at the boy in front of him. "Cora's son," he said.

"Fatherless?" Bert asked.

"Bastard," the old man said.

Bert's hands closed into fists, so the Colonel opened the drawer where the pistol was. He took it out and laid it on the table.

"You black bastard," he said.

"I've heard that before." Bert just stood there. "You're talking about my mother."

"Well," the Colonel answered, his fingers playing over the surface of the gun, "what can you do about it?"

The boy felt his whole body suddenly tighten and pull. The muscles of his forearms rippled.

"Niggers like you are hung to trees," the old man went on.

"I'm not a nigger," Bert said. "Ain't you my father? And a hell of a father you are, too, holding a gun on me."

"I'll break your black neck for you," the Colonel shouted. "Don't talk to me like that!" He jumped up.

"You'll break my neck?" The boy stood his ground as the father came toward him.

"Get out of here!" The Colonel shook with rage. "Get out! Or I'll do more than that if I ever lay eyes on you again." The old man picked up the pistol from the table, yet the boy did not move. "I'll fill you full of bullets if you come back here. Get off this place! Get to hell out of this county! Now, tonight. Go on!" The Colonel motioned with his pistol toward the door that led to the kitchen and the back of the house.

"Not that way," Bert said. "I'm not your servant. You must think I'm scared. Well, you can't drive me out the back way like a dog. You're not going to run me off, like a field hand you can't use any more. I'll go," the boy said, starting toward the front door, "but not out the back—from my own father's house."

"You nigger bastard!" Norwood screamed, springing between his son and the door, but the boy kept calmly on. The steel of the gun was between them, but that didn't matter. Rather, it seemed to pull them together like a magnet.

"Don't you . . .," Norwood began, for suddenly Bert's hand grasped the Colonel's arm, "dare put your . . .," and his old bones began to crack, "black hands on . . ."

"Why don't you shoot?" Bert interrupted him, slowly turning his wrist.

". . . me!"

"Why don't you shoot, then?"

The old man twisted and bent in fury and pain, but the gun fell to the floor.

"Why don't you shoot?" Bert said again as his hands sought his father's throat. With furious sureness they took the old white neck in their strong young fingers. "Why don't you shoot then, papa?"

Colonel Norwood clawed the air, breathing hoarsely and loud, his tongue growing stiff and dry, his eyes beginning to burn.

"Shoot—why don't you, then? Huh? Why?"

The chemicals of their two lives exploded. Everything was very black around them. The white man's hands stopped clawing the air. His heart stood still. His blood no longer flowed. He wasn't breathing.

"Why don't you shoot?" Bert said, but there was no answer.

When the boy's eyes cleared, he saw his mother standing at the foot of the stairs, so he let the body drop. It fell with a thud, old and white in a path of red from the setting sun.

"Why didn't he shoot, mama? He didn't want me

to live. He was white. Why didn't he shoot then?"

"Tom!" Cora cried, falling across his body. "Colonel Tom! Tom! Tom!"

"He's dead," Bert said. "I'm living though."

"Tom!" Cora screamed, pulling at the dead man. "Colonel Tom!"

Bert bent down and picked up the pistol. "This is what my father wanted to use on me," he said. "He's dead. But I can use it on all the white men in Georgia—they'll be coming to get me now. They never wanted me before, but I know they'll want me now." He stuffed the pistol in his shirt. Cora saw what her son had done.

"Run," she said, rising and going to him. "Run, chile! Out the front way quick, so's they won't see you in the kitchen. Make fo' de swamp, honey. Cross de fields fo' de swamp. Go de crick way. In runnin' water, dogs can't smell no tracks. Hurry, son!"

"Yes, mama," Bert said slowly. "But if I see they gonna get me before I reach the swamp, then I'm coming back here. Let them take me out of my father's house—if they can." He patted the gun inside his shirt, and smiled. "They'll never string me up to some roadside tree for the crackers to laugh at. Not me!"

"Hurry, chile," Cora opened the door and the sunset streamed in like a river of blood. "Hurry, chile."

Bert went out across the wide pillared porch and down the road. He saw Talbot and the storekeeper coming, so he turned off through the trees. And then, because he wanted to live, he began to run. The whole sky was a blaze of color as he ran. Then it began to get dark, and the glow went away.

In the house, Cora started to talk to the dead man on the floor, just as though he were not dead. She pushed and pulled at the body, trying to get him to get up himself. Then she heard the footsteps of Talbot and the storekeeper on the porch. She rose and stood as if petrified in the middle of the floor. A knock, and two men were peering through the screen door into the dusk-dark room. Then Talbot opened the door.

"Hello, Cora," he said. "What's the matter with you, why didn't you let us in? Where's that damn fool boy o' your'n goin', comin' out the front way liked he owned the place? What's the matter with you, woman? Can't you talk? Where's Colonel Norwood?"

"Let's have some light in here," said the storekeeper, turning a button beside the door.

"Great God!" Talbot cried. "Jim, look at this!" The Colonel's body lay huddled on the floor, old and purple-white, at Cora's feet.

"Why, he's blue in the face," the storekeeper said bending over the body. "Oh! Get that nigger we saw walking out the door! That nigger bastard of

Cora's. Get that nigger! . . . Why, the Colonel's dead!"

Talbot rushed toward the door. "That nigger," he cried. "He must be running toward the swamps now. . . . We'll get him. Telephone town, Jim, there in the library. Telephone the sheriff. Telephone the Beale family down by the swamp. Get men, white men, after that nigger."

The storekeeper ran into the library and began to call on the phone. Talbot looked at Cora standing in the center of the room. "Where's Norwood's car? In the barn? Talk, you black wench, talk!"

But Cora didn't say a word. She watched the two white men rush out of the house into the yard. In a few minutes, she heard the roar of a motor hurtling down the road. It was dark outside. Night had come.

Cora turned toward the body on the floor. "My boy," she said, "he can't get to de swamp now. They telephoned the white folks down that way to head him off. He'll come back home." She called aloud, "Colonel Tom, why don't you get up from there and help me? You know they're after our boy. You know they got him out there runnin' from de white folks in de night. Runnin' from de hounds and de guns and de ropes and all what they uses to kill poor niggers with. . . . Ma boy's out there runnin'. Why don't you help him?" Cora bent over the body. "Colonel Tom, you hear me? You said he was ma boy, ma bastard boy. I heard you. But he's your'n, too—out yonder in de dark runnin'—from your people. Why don't you get up and stop 'em? You know you could. You's a power in Polk County. You's a big man, and yet our son's out there runnin'—runnin' from po' white trash what ain't worth de little finger o' nobody's got your blood in 'em, Tom." Cora shook the dead body fiercely. "Get up from there and stop 'em, Colonel Tom." But the white man did not move.

Gradually Cora stopped shaking him. Then she rose and backed away from this man she had known so long. "You's cruel, Tom," she whispered. "I might a-knowed it—you'd be like that, sendin' ma boy out to die. I might a-knowed it ever since you beat him that time under de feet of de horses. Well, you won't mistreat him no more now. That's finished." She went toward the steps. "I'm gonna make a place for him. Upstairs under ma bed. He's ma chile, and I'll look out for him. And don't you come in ma bedroom while he's up there. Don't you come to my bed either no more a-tall. I calls for you to help me now, Tom, and you just lays there. I calls you to get up now, and you don't move. Whenever you called *me* in de night, I woke up. Whenever you wanted me to love you, I reached out ma arms to you. I bored you five children and now," her voice rose hysterically, "one of 'em's out yonder runnin' from your people. Our youngest boy's out yonder in de dark, runnin'! I 'spects you's out there, too, with de rest of de white folks. Uh-um! Bert's runnin' from *you*, too. You said he warn't your'n—Cora's po' little yellow bastard. But he is your'n, Colonel Tom, and he's runnin' from you. Yes, out yonder in de dark, you, *you* runnin' our chile with a gun in yo' hand, and Talbot followin' behind you with a rope to hang Bert with." She leaned against the wall near the staircase, sobbing violently. Then she went back toward the man on the floor. Her sobs gradually ceased as she looked down at his crumpled body. Then she said slowly, "Listen, I been sleepin' with you too long not to know that this ain't you, Tom, layin' down here with yo' eyes shut on de floor. You can't fool me— you ain't never been so still like this before—you's out yonder runnin' ma boy! Colonel Thomas Norwood runnin' ma boy through de fields in de dark, runnin' ma po' little helpless Bert through de fields in de dark for to lynch him and to kill him. . . . God damn you, Tom Norwood!" Cora cried, "God damn you!"

She went upstairs. For a long time the body lay alone on the floor in the parlor. Later Cora heard Sam and Livonia weeping and shouting in the kitchen, and Negro voices outside in the dark, and feet going down the road. She thought she heard the baying of hounds afar off, too, as she prepared a hiding place for Bert in the attic. Then she came down to her room and put the most beautiful quilts she had on her bed. "Maybe he'll just want to rest here first," she thought. "Maybe he'll be awful tired and just want to rest."

Then she heard a loud knock at the door, and white voices talking, and Sam's frightened answers. The doctor and the undertakers had come to take the body away. In a little while she heard them lifting it up and putting it in the dead wagon. And all the time, they kept talking, talking.

". . . 'll be havin' his funeral in town . . . ain't nothin' but niggers left out here . . . didn't have no relatives, did he, Sam? . . . Too bad. . . . Nobody to look after his stuff tonight. Every white man's able to walk's out with the posse . . . that young nigger'll swing before midnight . . . what a neck-tie party! . . . Say, Sam!"

"Yes, sah! Yes, sah!"

". . . that black housekeeper, Cora? . . . murderin' bastard's mother?"

"She's upstairs, I reckon, sah."

". . . like to see how she looks. Get her down here."

"Yes, sah!" Sam's teeth were chattering.

"And how about a little drink before we start back to town?"

"Yes, sah! Cora's got de keys fo' de licker, sah."

"Well, get her down, double quick, then!"

"Yes, sah!" Cora heard Sam coming up for her.

Downstairs, the voices went on. They were talking about her. ". . . lived together . . . ain't been a white woman here overnight since the wife died when I was a kid . . . bad business, though, livin' with a," in drawling cracker tones, "nigger."

As Cora came down the steps, the undertakers looked at her half-grinning. "So you're the black wench that's got these educated darkie children? Hum-m! Well I guess you'll see one of 'em swinging full o' bullet holes before you get up in the morning. . . . Or maybe they'll burn him. How'd you like a roasted darkie for breakfast, girlie?"

Cora stood quite still on the stairs. "Is that all you wanted to say to me?" she asked.

"Now, don't get smart," the doctor said. "Maybe you think there's nobody to boss you now. We're goin' to have a little drink before we go. Get out a bottle."

"I take ma orders from Colonel Norwood, suh," Cora said.

"Well, you'll take no more orders from him," the undertaker declared. "He's outside in the dead wagon. Get along now and get out a bottle."

"He's out yonder with de mob," Cora said.

"I tell you he's in my wagon, dead as a door nail."

"I tell you he's runnin' with de mob," Cora said.

"I believe this black woman's done gone nuts," the doctor cried. "Sam, you get the licker."

"Yes, sah!" Sam sputtered with fright. "Co-r-r-ra, gimme . . ."

But Cora did not move.

"Ah-a-a-a, Lawd hab mercy!" Sam cried.

"To hell with the licker, Charlie," the undertaker said nervously. "Let's start back to town. We want to get in on some of that excitement, too. They should've found that nigger by now—and I want to see 'em drag him out here."

"All right, Jim," the other agreed. Then, to Cora, "But don't you darkies go to bed until you see the bonfire. You all are gettin' beside yourselves around Polk County. We'll burn a few more of you if you don't watch out."

The men left and the wheels of the wagon turned on the drive. Sam began to cry.

"Hab mercy! Lawd Jesus, hab mercy! Cora, is you a fool? *Is* you? Then why didn't you give de mens de licker, riled as these white folks is? In ma old age, is I gonna be burnt by de crackers? Lawd, is I sinned? Lawd, what has I done?" He looked at Cora. "I sho ain't gonna stay heah tonight. I's gwine."

"Go on," she said. "The Colonel can get his own drinks when he comes back."

"Lawd God Jesus!" Sam, his eyes bucking from their sockets, bolted from the room fast as his old legs could carry him. Cora heard him running blindly through the house, moaning.

She went to the kitchen where pots were still boiling on the stove, but Livonia had fled, the biscuits burnt in the oven. She looked out the back door, but no lights were visible anywhere. The cabins were quiet.

"I reckon they all gone," she said to herself. "Even ma boy, Willie. I reckon he gone, too. You see, Colonel Tom, everybody's scared o' you. They know you done gone with de mob again, like you did that time they hung Luke Jordan and you went to help 'em. Now you's out chasin' ma boy, too. I hears you hollerin'."

And sure enough, all around the Big House in the dark, in a wide far-off circle, men and dog-cries and auto-horns sounded in the night. Nearer they came even as Cora stood at the back door, listening. She closed the door, bolted it, put out the light, and went back to the parlor. "He'll come in by de front," she said. "Back from de swamp way. He wont' let 'em stop him from gettin' home to me agin, just once. Po' little boy, he ain't got no place to go, no how. Po' boy, what growed up with such pride in his heart. Just like you, Colonel Tom. Spittin' image o' you. . . . Proud! . . . And got no place to go."

Nearer and nearer the man-hunt came, the cries and the horns and the dogs. Headlights began to flash in the dark down the road. Off through the trees, Cora heard men screaming. And suddenly feet running, running, running. Nearer, nearer. She knew it was him. She knew they had seen him, too.

Then there were voices shouting very near the house.

"Don't shoot, men. We want to get him alive."

"Close in on him!"

"He must be in them bushes there by the porch."

"Look!"

And suddenly shots rang out. The door opened. Cora saw flashes of fire spitting into the blackness, and Bert's tall body in the doorway. He was shooting at the voices outside in the dark. The door closed.

"Hello, Ma," he said. "One or two of 'em won't follow me no further."

Cora locked the door as bullets splintered through the wood, shattered the window panes. Then a great volley of shots struck the house, blinding head-lights focused on the porch. Shouts and cries of, "Nigger! Nigger! Get the nigger!" filled the night.

"I was waitin' for you, honey," Cora said. "Quick! Your hidin' place's ready for you, upstairs in de attic. I sawed out a place under de floor. Maybe they won't find you, chile. Hurry, 'fore your father comes."

"No time to hide, Ma," Bert panted. "They're at the door now. They'll be coming in the back way, too. They'll be coming in the windows. They'll be coming in everywhere. I got one bullet left, Ma. It's mine."

"Yes, son, it's your'n. Go upstairs in mama's room and lay down on ma bed and rest. I won't let 'em come up till you're gone. God bless you, chile."

Quickly, they embraced. A moment his head rested on her shoulder.

"I'm awful tired running, Ma. I couldn't get to the swamp. Seems like they been chasing me for hours. Crawling through the cotton a long time, I got to rest now."

Cora pushed him toward the stairs. "Go on, son," she said gently.

At the top, Bert turned and looked back at this little brown woman standing there waiting for the mob. Outside the noise was terrific. Men shouted and screamed, massing for action. All at once they seemed to rush in a great wave for the house. They broke the doors and windows in, and poured into the room—a savage crowd of white men, red and wild-eyed, with guns and knives, sticks and ropes, lanterns and flashlights. They paused at the foot of the stairs where Cora stood looking down at them silently.

"Keep still, men," one of the leaders said. "He's armed. . . . Say where's that yellow bastard of yours, Cora—upstairs?"

"Yes," Cora said. "Wait."

"Wait, hell!" the men cried. "Come on, boys, let's go!"

A shot rang out upstairs, then Cora knew it was all right.

"Go on," she said, stepping aside for the mob.

IX

The next morning when people saw a bloody and unrecognizable body hanging in the public square at the Junction, some said with a certain pleasure, "That's what we do to niggers down here," not realizing Bert had been taken dead, and that all the fun for the mob had been sort of stale at the end.

But others, aware of what had happened, thought, "It'd be a hell of a lot better lynching a live nigger. Say, ain't there nobody else mixed up in this here Norwood murder? Where's that boy's brother, Willie? Heh?"

So the evening papers carried this item in the late editions:

DOUBLE LYNCHING IN GEORGIA

A large mob late this afternoon wrecked vengeance on the second of two Negro field hands, the murderers of Colonel Thomas Norwood, wealthy planter found dead at Big House Plantation. Bert

Lewis was lynched last night, and his brother, Willie Lewis, today. The sheriff of the county is unable to identify any members of the mob. Colonel Norwood's funeral has not yet been held. The dead man left no heirs.

LANGSTON HUGHES was born in Joplin, Missouri, in 1902. After graduation from high school, he spent a year in Mexico with his father, then a year studying at Columbia University. His first poem in a nationally known magazine was "The Negro Speaks of Rivers," which appeared in *Crisis* in 1921. In 1926 he published his first book of poems, *The Weary Blues,* and received a scholarship at Lincoln University in Pennsylvania, where he won his B.A. in 1929. Poet, novelist, lecturer, playwright, Langston Hughes wrote more than thirty-five books, including *The Dream Keeper* (1932), *Shakespeare in Harlem* (1942), *Simple Speaks His Mind* (1950), *The Sweet Flypaper of Life* (1955), *Ask Your Mama* (1961), and *The Panther and the Lash,* a collection of poetry he put together before his death in 1967. His many fellowships and awards included a Guggenheim Fellowship in 1925, and a Spingarn Medal in 1960. In 1961 he was elected member of the National Institute of Arts and Letters.